TOMB

Rex Garland

ARTHUR H. STOCKWELL LTD
Torrs Park, Ilfracombe, Devon, EX34 8BA
Established 1898
www.ahstockwell.co.uk

First published in Great Britain, 2019

British Library Cataloguing-in-Publication Data.
A catalogue record for this book is available
from the British Library.

ISBN 978-0-7223-5007-2
Printed in Great Britain by
Arthur H. Stockwell Ltd
Torrs Park Ilfracombe
Devon EX34 8BA

ACKNOWLEDGEMENT

The enjoyment of reading this book is greatly enhanced by the front cover design and the black-and-white cartoons of

BIOGRAPHICAL DETAILS

The son of an advertising pioneer whose company spawned the large and highly successful Saatchi advertising empire, Rex Garland was educated at Charterhouse and 'The University of Life'. He founded his own filmsetting business in Bristol when hot metal was still the norm and was headhunted by Unilever to help introduce giant-sized ink-jet printing in Britain.

Rex was also an adventurer, including racing motorcycles, flying sailplanes for hundreds of hours around the south of England, and sailing at sea single-handed. Always a 'doer' but now physically handicapped, his present passion lies in writing.

FOREWORD

All these stories are from the author's pen. Only the first printed in this book has been previously published (by Audio Arcadia in *An Eclectic Mix Volume Five*).

All royalties due to the author of this paperback will be donated to the *Alzheimer's Society*. (*Registered Charity Number 296645*)

JUSTICE

For the last two years David has lived on *Justice*, his thirty-four-foot motorsailer, in a marina in the Solent, England. His Jewish birth name was Dawid Davidowitch. As a young man he had been a chef in Warsaw before the Second World War. He escaped arrest in 1940 because he was at work when the Nazis broke into the family home and dragged them all away: his father, a member of the Polish Socialist Party, his mother and his young sister, Dominika.

Dawid had been lucky that a neighbour phoned his friend, the head chef Stanislaw Warszawski, at the restaurant where he worked to report what had happened. Stanislaw was one of many brave Polish Catholics who were helping Jews to escape to England. The penalty for helping Jews was death. It is estimated that 50,000 Poles were murdered by the Nazis for this cause alone. When the German soldiers arrived at the restaurant Dawid had vanished, spirited to England. Stanislaw was bayoneted to death in front of the patrons.

When Dawid was told at the reception centre in Kent of those events back in his home town he shrieked in anguish. He had to be restrained as he thrashed around. He was held and treated in a secure mental institution for several weeks before being allowed to join the Pioneer Corps. He became a cook, then transferred to the newly formed Catering Corps. He did not reveal at this stage his recurring dreams, which became his avowed intent to find out what had happened to his family and to hunt down Stanislaw's killers, and exact his revenge.

Preferring now to be called David, he demonstrated his prodigious work ethic and dedication to the British, who had given him back his life. He learned the language, and rose through the ranks. He finished the war as a commissioned officer and after demobilisation held several jobs in London before becoming head waiter at the Dorchester Hotel Grill in London.

David spent every spare moment, both during the war and after, building files (literally boxes full) of information that might lead him to his lost family. He travelled around Europe in pursuit of his mission. He was advised by new friends he had made in the Polish community in London that it would be dangerous to travel to Poland in the early years after the war, for there was still much anti-Semitism in that country. The best hope that his family were alive came from an old woman he met in Berlin in 1950. She had been freed by the Russians from Treblinka camp in 1944. She could remember a girl about the same age as his sister with a name like Dominika Davidowitch, but she knew nothing about the mother or father. After nearly thirty years of relentless research the weight of the evidence he had collected pointed to Brazil as the place to continue his search.

He had fallen in love at the age of forty-seven with Anna, a housekeeper at the Dorchester Hotel. She was twelve years his junior and an orphan of Hungarian extract. She too was a Jew and shared with David the promise by Winston Churchill of British citizenship; for the Nazis had also sent thousands of Hungarian Jews to their deaths in extermination camps. In 1970 David and Anna married. She fanned the flames of his obsession to either find his family or seek the revenge he had planned.

And so they undertook the long flight to Rio de Janeiro, Brazil, via Dakar in Senegal, West Africa, for their honeymoon. Anna was thirty-seven years old when, just two days after they had arrived, she was killed by a bus in Rio de Janeiro. David's grief was made almost unbearable, not only by seeing her being struck as she crossed the street on an official crossing to join him on the other side, but then learning from the police that the driver had been drunk at the time, and, worst of all, that Anna had been pregnant.

The case did not go to court until two months after he had buried Anna in Rio. Because of their high regard for him, the Dorchester Hotel management granted David unlimited leave of absence until his affairs in Rio were settled. Marco Lopez was a detective and also witness for the prosecution at the bus driver's initial arrest and subsequent trial. Marco spoke good English. He and his wife insisted that David stay with them in their home as long as he wished. David marvelled for the second time in his life at the generosity given by a Christian family to a Jew.

He stayed with the Lopez family for the nine weeks until the bus driver came to trial. During that time David told Marco all he knew of the appalling events that took place in Warsaw the day he escaped in 1940. They became good friends. Marco spent much of his spare time helping David track clues as to his family's whereabouts in that vast country: to no avail. He knew that David would never achieve peace of mind until he had resolved what happened to his family during the war. He also feared what action David might take should it be that they had suffered the same fate as hundreds of thousands of other Jews under the Nazi regime.

David was disgusted and angry at the sentence given to the bus driver. For causing death by driving under the influence of alcohol and killing his dear Anna and their unborn child – a mere six years in jail. He returned to London. As head waiter in The Grill at the Dorchester for over thirty years, David knew many of the patrons of this prestigious restaurant. One regular luncheon visitor owned several hotels on the south coast. Hearing that David was approaching sixty-five years of age and retirement, he invited him to become the general manager of a hotel he had just bought in Southampton. David wanted to know how that job could fit with a plan he had for buying a boat and learning to sail. The diner then included in his offer an apartment in the hotel and a berth for his boat in a marina at Gosport, Portsmouth Harbour; his duties would include the housekeeping on the owner's yacht in the same marina. Such an offer could not be refused.

David signed a three-year contract. Over the next few weeks he tidied his affairs in London, sold his flat in Mayfair for a handsome profit and moved to Southampton. He enrolled on a course to learn about sailing and boat handling. His new boss helped him find a suitable craft, which he named *Justice*, for nothing could erase from his mind his lifelong mission to deliver justice as he saw it should his family have come to harm.

He enjoyed the challenge and hard work of those three

years, but at the end of his contract he could afford to take things easy. He left the hotel in Southampton with a generous bonus from his boss for a job well done. Together with his state pension and a private pension from his thirty-five years at The Dorchester he could retire to live on his boat.

Then a letter from Marco arrived: 'Phone me' was all it said, and he gave a phone number that was new to David. The year was 1990. David had plug-in mains electricity, a fridge and a TV on board his boat. He had the latest in mobile phones, which in those days was about the size of a breeze block. David called the number. They greeted each other as old friends do. David sensed an urgency behind Marco's voice.

Marco explained that he had recently interviewed a Mrs Dominika Schultz. She was of Polish extraction. He had told her about a Polish friend in England who many years back had travelled to Rio in search of his family and had spoken of a long-lost sister named Dominika. Mrs Schultz replied that Dominika was a common Polish name.

"However," continued Marco, "I am not allowed to discuss police business with you, but later her husband contacted me asking how he might get in touch with you. My training tells me to ask your permission before I pass on your details. My instinct tells me it would be in your interest if I did. What about it, old pal – yes or no?"

"Well, of course" was David's instant reply, and before he could utter another word Marco interrupted.

"That's all I wanted to hear, my friend. Destroy my letter and any evidence of this phone call or number. Don't contact me – I'll contact you. Bye."

And the line went dead.

David was left wondering if his lifelong search had finally come to an end. It had.

* * * * * * * * *

David and his sister were sat in the main saloon of his boat clasped in each other's arms, tears and sobs of joy making it impossible for more than a few gasped words. Gradually they calmed and forced themselves apart, looking at each other and shaking their heads from side to side. Reunited after fifty years. David was now sixty-nine and Dominika sixty-two – grey-haired ageing adults sharing their tears.

Their first faltering words had been in Polish, then David reverted to English. Her response, also in English, both amazed and delighted him. This brought out laughter from both of them, which in turn heightened a happiness they were experiencing for the first time in fifty years.

"This is Marco's doing, isn't it?" said David as they dried their tears.

"Sh-h-h-h, my dear brother," replied Dominika. "I have so much to tell you. Until Marco told me you were alive I had assumed that you also had become a victim of the Nazis all those years ago."

"How much time do you have?" David asked her.

"All the time in the world" was the reply.

On David's boat there were two separate sleeping cabins below deck, plus the heads, and a main saloon incorporating the galley. A large comfortable wheelhouse at deck level afforded a view across the harbour to Portsmouth. There was a toilet and shower block nearby. David immediately set about clearing the spare cabin of the piles of box files that held his collection of notes, newspapers and documents relating to his persistent preoccupation with the search for his family. As he worked he told his sister of his passion since that fateful day in 1940 when they were parted. He told her how he had dedicated his life to finding his family and how he would mete out justice should any one of them have come to harm at the hands of the Nazis. He begged her to tell him if she knew anything about their parents and how she had found him after so many years.

"Dawid, you must give me time and I will tell you for I too have been searching. I too have been driven by my emotions. You were lost, and now you are found again. I will share with you everything that I know. It will be as painful for you to hear as it will be for me to tell."

David realised that his mysterious phone conversation with Marco meant that he, Marco, had known more about his sister than he had revealed. From then on David's friends in the marina saw brother and sister in the wheelhouse every day in earnest conversation. He had told these friends of his lifelong search for the truth. Now he joyfully introduced Dominika to them, but there were no more invitations to them for drinks on deck or the occasional superb professionally prepared meal. It was assumed that the two of them had much catching up to do. And so they did.

Over the next few days Dominika related her horrific experiences from the moment she was dragged, together with her parents, out of their home in Warsaw to the Nazi extermination camp at Treblinka, to seeing their father beaten to death, and their mother die of typhus. Dominika herself had been raped and at first forced to work in the prison guards' kitchens. As David listened to her story he clenched his fists and could not hold back the tears.

In turn he told her how he had got to England, and of the anguish he experienced when learning of what took place in Warsaw on the day that he escaped. She told him that she had only survived by being selected to become a servant in the house of Nazi SS Commandant Hermann Klüger.

The wealthy Polish owners of the large house that the officer lived in just outside the camp had been 'disposed of'. Klüger's wife, Hanna, had been instrumental in saving Dominika from further personal abuse and provided her with a comparatively safe but hard life. Dominika was told she would be shot if she attempted to escape. She was authorised to visit the camp to get stores and was thus able to keep in contact with her mother and sometimes smuggle food to her; but as time went on she knew that Klüger was responsible for the deaths of her parents and thousands of others. It was this realisation that drove her desire to live long enough to exact her revenge.

She had been a virtual slave of the Klügers, forced to do all the menial tasks around the house under the supervision of the German housekeeper/cook. Only two things could remotely be called good: she ate well, because they all did in that house, and she learned the German language. Her room was a tiny converted pantry next to the basement kitchen, and she had use of an outside toilet which was frozen up for most of the winter.

One day in June 1944 she heard a rumour that Russian troops were only days away. In the camp she saw Herr Klüger and other SS guards loading works of art, clothing and food on to lorries and drive off into the forest. When she returned to the Commandant's house it was deserted. All the others had fled. Dominika, now aged sixteen, stayed to help the hundreds of young children whose parents had been slaughtered. She was caring for them when the Russians arrived.

Later a Polish infantry division of the British Army brought clothing, food, and doctors with medical supplies. With them also came a rabbi and his wife, who took her back to Kraków, in Poland, adopted her and treated her as if she was the gift from God they never thought they could have. They were not able to have children of their own and lavished everything they had upon Dominika.

Two years later these new and loving parents sent her to Kraków University, the greatest centre of learning in Poland. She studied languages. She chose Portuguese because the last thing she had heard her Nazi captors say was that they were headed for Lisbon. She also studied English, Spanish, German and French. She graduated with honours. She obtained a job as a language teacher in a Lisbon college and started the first part of her journey to track down the man she swore she would surely kill if she found him.

"So there I was in Lisbon," she told her brother, "a Polish Jew teaching French and German to Portuguese Catholic children!"

It was a joy for David to realise that despite everything his sister had been through she still maintained a sense of humour.

"Had I for one moment known that you were alive and in England," she continued, "my life might have taken a very different course."

Dominika recounted how she believed the task of recognising Herr Klüger would be made easier because of an old fencing scar just above his left eyebrow. Such scars were quite common among certain groups of Polish and German students of the 1920s (brought about by the practice of duelling known as 'academic fencing'). The students were proud of this mark of honour, but for Hermann Klüger it proved to be his nemesis.

It was eight years after she witnessed her enemy fleeing from the Russians that she was able to start her search. She put the story around the art dealers and auction houses of Lisbon that she was looking for an uncle who, she lied to them, like herself had been detained by the Nazis. She believed that he had escaped to Lisbon. She would not mention names, she said, because anti-Semitism was still rife in Europe. She explained that this uncle, an art dealer, had hidden his most valuable art treasures before the war and would almost certainly have tried to sell them under an assumed name.

Dominika continued: "It took another nine years before I finally found what I was looking for."

In 1960 she gleaned the information for which she had worked so hard. To her the identification was beyond doubt – of both Hermann and his wife.

An old art dealer, then in his eighties, told her that in 1944 a man he had at the time suspected was an ex-Nazi and who fitted her description had sold him several valuable paintings. This dealer told her how he felt that the war in Europe was of no concern to neutral Portugal. The seller had given his name as Walter Schmidt. He told the dealer that he and his wife were emigrating to Rio de Janeiro, Brazil, which has ancient ties with Portugal, and where he had a brother. The description of 'Walter Schmidt' fitted everything Dominika remembered about

Hermann Klüger, including the scar on his left temple.

"Thus I continued my journey for justice. If I had stopped to think what a vast country Brazil is," she said to David, "I might have been daunted by the task. Many Europeans were emigrating there; so armed with the art dealer's invaluable information, an excellent reference and a job waiting for me, I booked my passage and bade goodbye to my foster-parents in Kraków and friends in Lisbon.

"In 1961, aged thirty-three, my new life in Brazil began. I travelled to many parts of that huge country. The state-controlled education system was generous to teachers like myself. I was grateful for my years of experience in Lisbon, where my Portuguese language skills were honed to fluency – and, as you know, Portuguese is the native language of Brazil. However, illiteracy was widespread. Despite the fact that I went to that country to teach German and English, in the early days I found myself teaching the official Portuguese language to illiterate inland natives in some of the federal states that are many hundreds of miles from the big cities on the east coast."

David listened in awe to her narrative; his impatience was increasingly obvious.

"Looking at you now, my dear sister, over sixty though you may be," he said, "I can see that you must have been an attractive younger woman – you still have those looks. Why no male involvement?"

"I'm coming to that," she said. "From what you have told me about your own marriage, which ended in tragedy, I have been reluctant to tell you about mine, which until now has been the most wonderful thing to ever happen to me. Had I known about your visit to Rio things might have turned out so very differently."

David's tears welled up at the poignancy of her words – if only. He dived down into the galley to hide his emotions and emerged with more coffee for the two of them.

"Please," said David, "I know I have told you much about my life, but you say that you have news for me about that which has been haunting both of us most of our lives. I need to know every detail so that we can look to the future and decide what we are going to do next."

His sister continued: "I met Carl in Rio only a few years before you yourself travelled to that city. I was nearly forty and had landed a wonderful job as a lecturer in European languages at the Federal University of Rio de Janeiro, Brazil's oldest and most revered seat of learning.

"Carl is an American. His wife had died many years before I met him. His nineteen-year-old son was an undergraduate at my university, studying French and German as well as Portuguese. His father came to see me to enquire how his son was progressing. I know it's an old cliché, as you say, but it really was love at first sight for both of us. I tried hard to convince myself about my real goal in life, but I could not resist this final chance of personal happiness.

"Carl was someone on whom I unburdened my innermost thoughts. As if by some amazing coincidence, or what Christians call a miracle, it transpired that he had a special understanding of my search for revenge. You see, Carl, several years older than myself, of German Jewish extraction, had been with the USA armed forces during the war and afterwards was horrified to learn of the evils of the Nazis when he was a guard at the Nuremberg trials. His sympathy for my quest was every bit as strong as mine.

"And so I became Mrs Carl Schultz. Carl had originally

gone to Brazil as a technician for a Californian private swimming-pool company and now owned his own successful business – Schultz Pools Inc. Brazil is a country of great inequality between the rich and the poor. Tax evasion, gunrunning, drugs, fraud and corruption were then on a massive scale. Carl's son Joseph's ambition was to join his father's company.

"With a great deal of help from me, including extra tuition at home, it is not surprising he scored well with his degree. The business went from strength to strength. Joseph's language skills gave him an advantage as a salesman when it came to dealing with the nouveau riche of Rio, many of whom came from Europe speaking limited Portuguese. The considerable wealth of many of these people was of dubious origin.

"Carl and I loved our jobs and our lives together have been happy. Although as the years went by we talked less frequently about my mission, neither of us lost the burning desire to mete out justice if we could. We both continued to make discreet enquiries. We also agreed not to divulge our thoughts on these matters to anyone – especially Joseph, who by 1975 was twenty-eight, married, and had taken over our old colonial-style house just outside Rio. The company demonstration swimming pool was there. Carl and I had an apartment near Copacabana Beach, close to the campus where I worked. Though I say it myself, at forty-seven I still had a decent figure and Carl was always telling me I could compete with the best on the beach!"

"It sounds like everybody's dream," said David.

"In a way it was, brother dear, especially now Carl and I were on our own. The registered office of the business was at our old house, with Joseph in charge of sales, demonstrations and maintenance. Joseph's wife was his personal assistant, and he was responsible for five full-time engineers. Private swimming pools are luxury items and cost a lot of money, not just to have built but also to maintain safely.

"Carl's priority was to ensure that safety regulations concerning the design, building and maintenance were observed. He supervised every build and installation, and got to know all the customers. It was his responsibility to ensure they knew the inherent dangers of pool ownership. I tell you all this so that you will better understand what happened a few months ago."

Despite his impatience to hear the conclusion of his sister's story, David insisted that she should see something of the country that had been so good to him. One day they took the ferry across the harbour to Portsmouth, where Dominika marvelled at the sights recalling England's ancient naval history. Laden with fresh stores and with David's promise to cook a traditional Polish meal, they returned to the boat for an evening of nostalgia, and finally the truth.

* * * * * * * * * *

David asked his sister to stay in the wheelhouse whilst he exercised his culinary skills in the galley below. He called her down to the main saloon, where the pierogi dumplings stuffed with sauerkraut, pork, mushrooms and cheese brought back family memories. After their meal Dominika sensed that this was the time to finish her story. Armed with two glasses and a large bottle of the Polish mead that David always kept on board they climbed back up into the wheelhouse. As the night fell, lit only by the lights from the pontoon, the city of Portsmouth reflected on the calm water across the harbour, Dominika spoke to her brother in a hushed tone as if she feared someone might overhear.

"It was not uncommon for Carl to be away. His customers could be hundreds of miles from Rio. He might not be back for several days. Some districts were well served by the nationalised railways. One day he left to take an early train long before I went to work. The detective who was waiting for me when I returned from the campus that evening wanted to know Carl's whereabouts. I couldn't tell him; nor did I know when Carl would be back. Of course I wanted to know why he was asking all these questions."

"He explained that he was investigating the reason why a local man had broken his neck that afternoon; the only word he had spoken in hospital was 'Schultz'. There seemed little doubt that his injury came from diving into his pool, which contained insufficient water to prevent him hitting the bottom. After the detective had left I phoned Joseph. His wife said that Joseph had been asked to go to the police station – and no, she didn't know where her father-in-law was either. I had a lot of preparation work to do that evening for my student lecture in the morning, but I was naturally worried and felt sorry for the man in hospital."

"Later that evening it came as a terrible shock when I received a phone call from the police to say that Carl had been arrested and was being held at the local police station. I jumped into the car, but when I arrived at where he was being held they would not let me see him. I went home and after phoning our solicitor spent a sleepless night worrying as to how Carl or his company could possibly be held responsible for a pool owner's injuries.

Carl, looking very shaken, arrived back at the apartment early the next morning driven by our solicitor."

"And the name of the detective who came to see you?" David almost shouted at her.

"Marco Lopez," she replied with a smile.

"Over breakfast Carl told me that Alberto Mendes, the pool owner, had phoned Joseph a few days earlier requesting someone to call about an algae problem. First thing the following day Joseph sent one of their engineers to investigate. This man advised the owner that it was necessary to partly drain the pool, which he did."

Dominika went on to explain that this engineer was the first to be questioned by the police. He told them that before he left the premises he explained to Mr Mendes why, for safety reasons, he had bolted the door from the pool to the garden from the inside, double-locked the entry door from the house, and deposited the keys in the pump house outside. The engineer showed the police his written report, in which he had noted that *'This foreign gentleman nodded his understanding of my actions, but I thought his Portuguese was not good.'*

"Carl tried hard to dissuade me from visiting the hospital to see the injured man, who I had been told was about seventy-five years old with no known relatives and unlikely to survive more than a few days. I went nevertheless. He lay in bed with a steel frame fastened around his head, his upper torso and hands swathed in bandages, life-support monitors quietly bleeping alongside.

"The nurse introduced me as I had asked: 'Dominika to see you, Mr Mendes.'

"I peered into his face. Slowly, with absolute certainty of mind I leaned close to his ear.

"'Hello, Herr Klüger. Remember me?' I said in German. For there before me lay Hermann Klüger, alias Walter Schmidt, alias Alberto Mendes."

"Good God!" exclaimed David. "How could you be so sure after forty-five years?"

"The moment I entered the room and he heard my name I saw the look of recognition in his eyes as he noticed mine drawn to the scar on his left temple, which was visible above his sparse grey eyebrow. As soon as I saw it I knew why Carl had been opposed to me visiting the hospital."

"My mind raced to little things that Carl had mentioned in previous weeks. Then I had doubts about the timetable with which Carl told me he had satisfied the police concerning his movements on the day of the accident. Finally, I saw the fear in the patient's face, and I knew."

"Klüger's eyes turned moist as he mumbled, '*Verzeih mir, mein Kind*' (Forgive me, my child) as the tears rolled down his cheeks. What I saw at that moment was an old man in great pain begging me for that which only I could give."

'*Ich vergebe,*' I answered.

"Seconds after I had spoken those two words his eyes closed and the bleeps on the monitors changed to a high-pitched continuous tone. The nurse and a doctor rushed into the room; I turned directly to them and spoke in Portuguese: 'Do not resuscitate.' He was certified dead within minutes."

David screamed in fury, "We were cheated! No! No!" He violently shook his fists in the air.

"Please, dear brother, vengeance has destroyed two lives already. We have found each other. Let us return to happiness and look forward, not back. Carl says you are welcome to our home any time – and Marco Lopez says that the same goes for him."

OLD TIMERS

Two shabby and bearded old men sitting at either end of a small bench in St James's Park, Central London. One, his gnarled hands on a sturdy stick, the other, his pipe barely alight. One muttered a few words about the weather; the other turned to peer more closely at his neighbour.

"Aven't I seen you somewheres before, mate?"

"Only if you'm been visiting Her Majesty's premises," replied Peter in his distinctive West Country accent.

George thought that maybe this guy might just be referring to nearby Buckingham Palace, or 'Buck House' as it was irreverently called by some. He also thought he'd heard that accent before.

George shuffled along the bench until he was close up to this fellow scruff and whispered. "I bet you could tell a tale or two."

"Ooh arghh," said Peter as he resumed sucking on his empty pipe. "Ain't got no baccy by chance, have ee?"

George delved into an inner pocket of his tatty old jacket and offered him a worn brown leather pouch.

"'Elp y'self."

"Ta" was the reply.

Peter filled his pipe carefully before handing back the pouch.

"Light?"

Once again George reached inside his jacket, and this

time he produced an old battered brass Zippo with an engraving of a dragon breathing fire on one side. The effect on Peter as he took the lighter was amazing. One glance and he turned to fling his arms around his companion.

"Well, I'm buggered!" he cried. "'Tis me old mate George the Forge. Remember me? Peter the Pocket. Thought I knew that voice. Traded you this old lighter in exchange for some false discharge papers, I did an' all. Must 'ave been Brixton Prison, thir'y year ago an' all."

"Now I remember," replied George thoughtfully and, after a long pause, "Took me a long time an' all did them papers."

"Trouble was them papers weren't as smart as you do say," continued Peter. "Oh dear no! Oy be rearrested the moment I step outside the gates. Transferred me, they did, to Wormwood Scrubs wi' six months added for attempting an escape."

A period of silence ensued as Peter lit his pipe with the old Zippo, tapping down the glowing tobacco with the base of the lighter, which he looked at, nodding his head up and down slowly as if greeting an old friend; then he handed it back. Leaning over and giving George another long hug, he heaved himself up from the bench. Before he hobbled off he tapped George gently on the arm with his stick.

"No 'ard feelings though," he mumbled.

George watched Peter limp away toward The Mall and breathed a sigh of relief as he thought how lucky he had been that Peter never knew that he had double-crossed him. For George had tipped off one of the prison guards about the false papers on that day thirty years ago in return for the restoration of his own lost privileges.

George's way home was to leave the park in the

opposite direction along Birdcage Walk, leading to aptly named Great George Street, through Parliament Square, past Big Ben and across Westminster Bridge to where he caught his bus back to the hostel on the south side of the Thames. As he approached the bus stop and reached inside his jacket he realised that he was no longer in possession of the old battered lighter, the tobacco pouch, his pocket watch and his wallet containing his bus pass and a tenner.

FUEL, SERVICE AND MOT
SUPER

CZECH MATE

Soon after John Taphstein had bought his home on the south coast and registered as a patient with Peter Featherstone, MD, he found himself one weekend talking to his new doctor in the bar of their local golf club. When Dr Featherstone learned from John that he was in the flower business, and in particular that his company was based at The New Flower Market at Nine Elms, London, he told him that his seventeen-year-old daughter and only child, Amy, had been mad about flowers ever since she had stayed with her Aunt Joan in London and visited New Covent Garden last year, and that she was now looking for a job.

"Her luck might be in," John had replied. "I don't make these decisions myself, but my market manager mentioned he was looking for an assistant. I'll phone him when I get home." He handed Peter a card. "Give David Arnott a ring on Monday morning and tell him you and I have been having a chat."

Early one morning a week later saw Amy and her father hugging on the platform at Chichester Station as the train for London came in. As it departed he gave her the thumbs-up sign and she grinned happily at him out of the window. She was on her way to her first job interview.

"I've got it, Daddy!" she cried out the moment she entered the front door when she arrived home late that same evening.

"I knew you would," called her father from the kitchen. "Come out here – see what I have prepared for our celebration. My surgery finished early tonight."

There on the big oak kitchen table was a spread of cold lobster, prawns, potato salad and coleslaw.

"Champagne and ice cream in the fridge," he continued as she ran into the room.

She grabbed her father around the neck and gave him a big kiss. It was the first time since her mother had died only a year ago that Peter had seen a look of real happiness on his daughter's face.

"And now for another piece of good news, my beautiful girl. I've spoken to Aunt Joan, and she would love you to stay with her during the week if that's what you would like."

"Like? Dad, that's wonderful. It was only when I was in the train on the way home that I started to wonder how I was going to get to work in London at five o'clock every morning! That's when they start."

"I wouldn't have suggested you went for the interview if I hadn't spoken to my sister first," he revealed. "Now you can walk to work."

This time Amy burst into tears, for Aunt Joan lived near Battersea Park, less than a mile away from the market. Exhausted from emotion, excitement, and perhaps a little too much champagne, it was not long after the end of the meal and much speculation about the job that they climbed the stairs to their bedrooms. It was the first occasion for a very long time that laughter had been heard in that house.

Over breakfast Amy said to her father with a smirk, "Who's going to look after you when I'm not here?"

But she knew very well how independent he was, even though she – and her mum when she was alive – had done all of the cooking and housekeeping. With his surgery in the large house next door, which he shared with four other partners, she knew that her dad would be fine, and that they would be together at weekends.

But not for very long. A mere eighteen months later Amy and John Taphstein were married. Amy had kept her father posted about their growing romance, but Peter had become much more inquisitive when John proposed marriage. For a start there was an age difference of nearly twenty years, making John twice her age. Peter also tried to extract from John information about his previous marriage, but John told him it was too painful to talk about the death of his wife many years ago and the subsequent falling-out with his young son, who he said had recently emigrated to Australia in order to join his girlfriend.

Amy became Mrs Taphstein on her nineteenth birthday. John gave her everything she had ever dreamed about: tender affection, a charming home, a job and security. She had the blessings of her father, for he had found no reason to stand in their way despite his earlier misgivings and discreet enquiries he had made at the golf club.

By the time she was twenty-five Amy had learned a great deal about the trade during the seven years she worked at Taphstein's, both before and after their marriage. She loved her job and was liked by the staff. On weekdays they lived at John's flat near The Oval cricket ground, which was very convenient because they both had to be in the flower market at five in the morning. At weekends they drove down to their old Sussex farmhouse home. Father and son-in-law played golf together.

Peter was delighted when, as a surprise for her twenty-fifth birthday, John handed Amy the deeds of a property he had purchased in her old home town overlooking Chichester Harbour, a few miles from their Sussex farmhouse. It consisted of a double-fronted shop with accommodation on the two floors above. She had long wanted her own business. Now here it was. It was all hers to make what she could of it, and having a tenant in the flat above would contribute to its viability. The sign above the shop windows – pink with a gold script outline – read:

'Amy's – New Covent Garden'

For Amy, no more commuting to London. This new interest also kept her very busy during her husband's frequent trips abroad. The shop was open seven days a week. Even though John was now spending only two or three days a week at the market he retained his Battersea flat. He said the London flat was convenient for overnight stopovers, for early meetings in the market or when he visited suppliers in Europe. John would fly from London City Airport to the Netherlands, France, the Channel Islands or Ibiza. Approaching fifty, he was now a wealthy man.

Amy at thirty years of age was a handsome woman indeed. Her auburn hair retained its colour and lustre as it had been when she was a teenager. It hung in a long ponytail, which reached to her waist. She had kept her slim figure, helped perhaps by the fact that she had not borne children. Her skin was clear and smooth, her eyes a Cambridge blue that always seemed to sparkle, and the dimples when she smiled contributed to the impression that she was flirting with whomever she addressed – an asset that charmed not just her customers, but all who met her.

Amy's flower shop thrived. Her distinctive little pale-green Citroën delivery van was easily recognised by all, with its hand-painted flowers on the corrugated body panels. Her variety of garden goods and flowers came straight from Taphstein's. There was no shortage of events at grand houses and estates nearby requiring fresh flower arrangements, and her planting-out stock competed with garden centres. She was immensely proud that her contribution to such a successful marriage included a part in their enviable financial position. And, of course, she could see her father any time.

It didn't happen with just one event. Peter Featherstone combined a holiday in Australia with a medical convention in Sydney. Whilst in Sydney he had looked in the local phone directory for the name Taphstein. He was curious about his daughter's stepson. There was just the one entry to call.

"Taphstein," declared the female voice that answered the phone.

Peter assumed he was talking to the son's wife or partner. He asked to speak to Mr Taphstein.

"If you want to talk to that bastard bigamist you need to go to London, England," came the reply, and the line went dead.

Peter was shocked. He assumed that she was talking about John's son. Knowing that John hadn't wanted the subject aired, he didn't immediately mention the incident to either him or Amy when he returned to the UK.

On the Friday following his return, during a rare visit to London to see his sister, Joan, Peter called afterwards at The Oval flat in the hope that John could throw some light on his mysterious Sydney phone call. An attractive young woman came to the front door to say that she was the cleaner and nobody else was at home. He'd seen this person before somewhere. Driving home he thought he remembered where, and bells started to ring in his head.

"Hello, darling," Peter called out to his daughter as he entered her shop the next morning. "I have an ulterior reason for coming to see you."

Amy introduced her assistant, Laura, and explained that Annemarie was away for a couple of days. One glance at the photo on the wall of three smiling women holding a 'Florist of the Year' award confirmed to Peter that one of them was Annemarie, the girl he'd seen at the flat in London the day before.

Without revealing his deepening concern, he voiced his 'ulterior' reason for calling: "Darling, you once told me that the flat upstairs had a view out across the harbour. I was thinking that a few years from now, when I retire, if it became vacant it might do me very nicely – especially with you as the landlady!" He said this with as broad a smile as he could muster.

"Unusually for a Saturday," Amy grinned back, "I just this moment saw Jan go round. Come with me."

They went out of the shop, down the lane at the side and up the outside iron staircase to the flat entrance.

Jan (pronounced Yan) Holik was the son of the local Czechoslovakian-born motor trader and garage owner. Jan first came to Peter's attention in his surgery one day years ago when he and Amy were at school together. The boy had come round to declare his undying love for Amy and wanted her father's permission to take her out. At the time Peter had been struck by his old-fashioned courtesy.

After leaving school the two young people went their own ways. Jan graduated from Southampton University with a professional diploma in information technology and, as we know, Amy went to London. Whilst working at his father's garage Jan had helped many of their customers, including Dr Featherstone, with computer problems. His declared aim was to set up his own IT consultancy one day. It had been no surprise to Peter when Jan became Amy's tenant above the flower shop.

At the top of the outside stairs Amy rang the doorbell. When Jan opened the door, his eyebrows rose as she spoke.

"Sorry to trouble you, Jan. I wanted to show my dad the flat. He's never seen it. Is it convenient for us to come in for a few minutes and have a look around?"

"Hello, Dr Featherstone. Nice to see you again. By all means," said Jan, and waved them in.

The flat consisted of an entry vestibule with a cloakroom on one side and the staircase up to the top floor on the other; straight ahead was a large double bedroom and en-suite bathroom. With a wave of his hand and the brief description "My bedroom," he ushered them up the stairs, led by Amy. He followed a few seconds later. Peter was certain that the glimpse of a photo he had seen by the bedside was of his daughter. As he climbed the stairs he was assailed with a confusion of thoughts.

"Step warily," he cautioned himself as they entered the top floor.

At one end of this large area, with windows on three

sides and furnished as a modern sitting room, was a breakfast bar and fully fitted kitchen, with a separate toilet at the back. Most of the south side consisted of two pairs of wide patio-type doors leading on to a balcony which gave a view over the flat roof of the only building between them and the water, right across Chichester Harbour and out to sea three or four miles away.

"It's stunning," declared Peter as he stepped out on to the balcony.

"Don't say any more, sir," cried Jan, "or Amy will put the rent up!"

Amy repeated to Jan what her father had said in the shop about retirement.

Jan raised his eyebrows in a questioning mode, but there was also a smile. Looking straight at Amy he retorted, "So you'd throw me out, would you?"

They all laughed.

Peter detected a sense of intimacy between the two of them. As he and Amy left the flat he looked again into the bedroom and noticed that the photo beside the bed had been moved to face-down.

"Oh, how's John?" said Peter to his daughter when they had returned downstairs to the shop.

"Fine, as far as I know," she replied somewhat unconcernedly. "He left for Amsterdam on Thursday, saying he would not be back until Monday or Tuesday. He's negotiating with a new tulip supplier, I think."

Peter kept his thoughts to himself as he said his goodbyes and left.

After a sleepless night at home he decided to drive the

short distance to his daughter's house the next morning.

He was greeted with "Come in, Daddy. Annemarie is here. I can't remember if you two have met before."

As the two of them entered the living room it is difficult to say who looked the most surprised on being introduced, Annemarie or Peter.

After an awkward pause Annemarie threw her arms around Amy. "Oh, Amy, I didn't know it was your dad," she cried out.

Amy looked quizzical, and an even longer silence followed before Peter spoke: "Can someone please tell me what's going on here?"

Amy prised Annemarie's arms from around her, turned quickly to her father and gently led him to the sofa.

"Daddy, I've tried hard not to worry you."

"Worry doesn't come into it," said Peter in exasperation. "I saw this young lady in your London flat only two days ago. She said she was the cleaner. Well?"

"Oh, Daddy, Annemarie has been collecting evidence for me. She and Jan are my best friends. Now I know for sure that John is – is a bigamist and a cheat. For years he has been lying to me. I loved him, Daddy. Oh, how I loved him."

She collapsed sobbing into her father's arms. He held her tightly.

"I was just his weekend girl," she cried in anguish as the tears flowed.

Her story came pouring out, but of course Peter needed no convincing. He'd spoken to the other Mrs Taphstein himself, hadn't he? He controlled his rising anger. He listened to how Amy, who had known for a long time that Jan was still in love with her, had at first rejected his suggestion that her husband was not being faithful. Peter listened to how Jan had secretly planted a GPS tracker in John's car whilst it was in the Holiks' garage for a service. It was not parked at the airport as John had said during weekends when he was supposed to be in Europe. It was at The Oval flat. Then she explained Annemarie's visit to the flat last week.

When they were certain that John was abroad, Annemarie went up to The Oval flat and discovered evidence that there had been another woman there, and that there was yet another in Amsterdam. Now Peter realised it was the first Mrs Taphstein he had spoken to in Sydney – and that there never had been a son.

* * * * * * *

The Taphstein Sussex residence, Downs Farm, a beautifully modernised Edwardian farmhouse set in twenty acres, was at the end of a long private drive up a valley in the foothills of the South Downs. The large thatched barn, away from the house, served as a garage for John's car, Amy's van, a sit-on motor mower and other garden machinery.

On the Saturday in question it must have been alight for a long time before a passing motorist on the main road a mile away noticed flames above the surrounding trees and called the fire service. The timber framing and thatched roofing of the barn had collapsed on to the contents beneath. It was another hour before the fire was sufficiently damped down to allow them to comb through the smouldering debris.

Evidence at the coroner's inquest revealed that Mr Taphstein, after golf in the morning, had participated in a particularly liquid lunch with his golfing partner. What was not revealed was that another club member, one of

Dr Featherstone's patients, had phoned Peter from the clubhouse that day to say he was worried about Peter's son-in-law driving home. Peter had replied that he would deal with the matter right away and asked for his patient's discretion not to mention the phone call to anyone, which of course, at his doctor's request, he never did.

The evidence also indicated that John, on leaving the golf club after lunch, drove to the Holiks' garage and purchased fuel; and as well as filling the car he had filled several plastic containers. He had then driven off in the direction of his home. The pump attendant could not see from his window how much petrol went into the car or how much into the containers, but John's total purchase was far in excess of the car's own tank capacity.

Jan Holik's evidence was that he had, on a previous occasion – he couldn't remember when – warned Mr Taphstein that his containers were not suitable for the transporting of petrol, but on this occasion he was in the workshop of the garage and was not aware of John's visit. Annemarie and Amy's evidence showed that they were at the time very busy in the shop or at the back packing orders, delivering and serving all that day. They were seen together by many customers.

John Taphstein was assumed to have parked his car in the barn after arriving home and fallen asleep at the wheel. His inebriation accounted for the reason why all the doors were found locked, the keys in the ignition. On waking he must have tried to light a cigarette and, by so doing, ignited the fumes from insecurely closed containers which were in the well of the back seats because his clubs and trolley had filled the boot. The resulting explosion would have been instantaneous and fatal for any occupant.

The molten remains of his gold cigarette lighter were found among the ashes of his totally incinerated body in the driver's seat. He could only be identified from dental records. There was no evidence after such an intense fire to suggest anything other than a verdict of accidental death. Interestingly no one asked who else might've had a spare ignition key.

"Darling, would you like me to confirm it for you?" Dr Featherstone was answering a phone call which he had been warned by his daughter to expect.

"No need, Daddy – the clinic are certain. I haven't told Jan yet – you are the first to know."

"Just remember, darling, our agreement that weekend when I first saw the flat? I am ready to move in when you two have got your act together. That flat is not suitable even to prepare to have children."

"Daddy, I didn't call you to remind you of any agreement."

"I know, my darling. That is one matter between us I suggest we all forget, and which definitely does not need to be put in writing. But for legal requirements the gift of my house deeds to you as a wedding present and my tenancy of the flat for life do. You two have rightly decided not to live in a house with unhappy memories. So sell it whenever you see fit. Your arrangement with the other Mrs Taphstein in Australia to share the proceeds fifty-fifty meets with my full approval. I'm glad I tracked her down for you. Furthermore, the sooner I can have a room with a view the better. Be positive. Look forward. Put the Taphstein years behind you. They have not been too much of a loss, have they? In fact you could say that recent events have led to better fortune in the future for you, me and however many Holiks there are to come."

PLEASE

> Please mum, sorry to ask again. Lost my card this time as well as mobile. They wiped me out. Had to buy new phone and get new bank a/c, details as follows. 10-58-22, account No.109738652. Anything will do. Don't get paid by farm shop till next month – thanks, luv John

Emily's jaw dropped as she read the latest text from her son, pushed the mobile back into her purse and turned to her friend Mary.

"Not again," she said to her best friend and neighbour as they rattled round the supermarket together during their lunch break. "Does yours keep losing things at university, Mary?"

"All the time. She's absolutely hopeless. At first I thought maybe her room-mates were nicking the stuff. At this rate she'll need to get a job as a brain surgeon after she graduates to pay off all the debts! Time for a coffee, Emily? Come on."

As Emily slurped the coffee, her normally happy face looked worried and distracted.

To change the subject her friend said, "Have you and David sorted out that old banger of yours?"

"No, not yet. I know David gets requests for money from John just as I do and doesn't always tell me, same as I don't tell him. We seem to silently agree that we just haven't got the money to spend on a new car. Even John himself told us in the summer that we were the laughing stock of the neighbourhood."

Mary leaned across the table and lowered her voice: "Emily, love, you are the best friend I've ever had in my whole life. If I don't open my mouth and something happens I'll never forgive myself."

Mary noticed Emily's brow furrow deeper still.

"What do you mean – if something happens?"

"We heard you two from the garden the other evening," Mary continued. "Your back door was open – we could hear every word."

Emily shot her hand across her mouth, with her eyes now opened wide.

"Please, Emily, listen to me. Your marriage is heading for the rocks. Whatever you think you are doing for your son will mean nothing if by the time he graduates he comes back to a broken home."

Tears were now rolling down Emily's flushed cheeks as she reached into her purse for a tissue and sobbed.

"You heard everything, then – everything?"

"Yes, Emily, love. Robert and I have been worried sick ever since. We understand about the car – you only have the one and it means everything to you. You and David met as a result of your passion for motoring. When John was a child you toured as a family. That car was your escape. Even polishing it on a Sunday morning together was part of your lives. If your son got so much as a whisper of what I heard you two had in mind he'd quit university immediately to get any old job to help you out."

"We've stretched ourselves", stuttered Emily as she

wiped away her tears, "to give John the best chance in life."

"I know, Emily, my dear friend, but there is no way I can allow you to prostitute yourself to that toad."

"What are we going to do, then, Mary? Got any better ideas?"

"Yes. Turn the tables on that loathsome Mr Trurnbull. I've had a similar experience and approach from him. He very nearly rejected our mortgage application years ago. He clearly has been behaving like that for years. Listen to me – this is what you do. . . ."

The money that Emily spent in the beauty parlour left her feeling years younger. She looked stunning. With her golden curly hair framing her pretty face, she made her way to the appointment at the bank. As she sat down opposite Mr Trurnbull in his office she placed her purse facing him on his desk. After delving into it, ostensibly to remove a small handkerchief, she adjusted her unusually short skirt as she crossed her shapely legs.

"I've been thinking about what you said the last time we met, Mr Trurnbull." Emily lowered her voice as she leaned across the bank manager's desk and looked concernedly at the door leading to his secretary's office. "My husband has gone away for a few days."

"It's all right, Mrs Johnson, this is a totally private conversation. And please call me George." He smiled and did not hide the reason for moving his chair – for a better look at her legs.

"You must understand, Mr – er – George, that this is strictly business." Not waiting for a reply Emily continued: "Your wife should now be visiting her relations in Canada this week, you told me, yes? Is that right?" This time she did pause.

"That is absolutely right. Emily, if I might be so bold . . ."

He placed his elbows on the desk, steepled his fingers together and placed his lips on them, eyes lowered in apparently deep concentration. What seemed like an eternity to Emily passed. Then he reached forward, grasped her purse and, to her horror, pulled it across the desk close to him and dropped it into the top drawer.

"This is what we'll do, Emily," he continued with a grin: "I shall call my secretary in and instruct her to prepare the usual letter and bank documents that authorise the overdraft you requested. So now you will have your proof as to the bank's intentions. Because of the urgency that you have expressed to conclude the transaction I will, early tomorrow morning, personally, on my way to the bank, bring the letter of authorisation round to your house, where you can sign the forms. Perhaps in the bedroom?"

"And", he said with an even more exaggerated grin, "you will be pleased to know that I shall also bring with me the purse that you accidentally left behind in your rush to go home today and celebrate your good news. It will of course no longer contain the voice recorder which you have switched on."

Emily looked shocked and embarrassed, but before she could say another word George Trurnbull had pressed the bell on his desk and his secretary entered immediately.

"It's all right, Miss Draper," he said as his secretary looked startled at the customer's demeanour. "Mrs Johnson is overcome by the bank's decision that means she can now purchase the new family car."

Mary waited in her car outside until she saw Emily leave the bank to catch the bus home from the stop on the other side of the road. On being reunited in Mary's kitchen, they hugged and kissed before sitting down to their coffee and two very large glasses of wine.

Mary raised her glass. "Good thing we decided on belt and braces. I knew he wouldn't suspect a brooch microphone as well. Here's to Wi-Fi, Bluetooth and the rest. You can imagine I breathed a sigh of relief when I got there early and found the space empty in the bank's private car park right outside his office window. From there on everything went like clockwork."

Emily's pretty face broke into a smile. "I was nervous as hell," she said. "Good thing you warned me what could happen, Mary. When I coloured up in his office I thought it was all over."

"All over, my foot!" replied Mary as she topped up their glasses. "The fun is only starting. This is where you not only prove your acting ability and get your new car, but we'll have that slimy toad eating from our hands. Just make sure, my dearest friend, that (a) in the morning you are at your most seductive, and (b), preferably when he's got his trousers down," she added, giggling, "you insist that to honour his agreement he first hands you the bank's letter and papers that you've both just signed. Then you drop them into a drawer in your dressing table, which you lock, depositing the key into a vase of flowers."

"Now for the fun bit. You then play to dear George the copy of our recording at the bank this morning and tap your phone to dial my number. After he has left, which you can be sure will be in a great hurry when he hears me not only ring your front-door bell but shout through the letter box that I'll be up in a few minutes using my own key in case you are in the shower, we will both then be able to enjoy at our leisure the look on his face, or, even more, taken by the video camera hidden in your powder box!"

NO BOUNDS

His assumption that he was destined to a lonely life changed when David found a pen pal in Mississippi, USA. He fell in love with Mary by email. Every day for nearly two years they exchanged their innermost thoughts and longings. They became true soulmates. Apart nearly halfway round the world, David longed for the day they would be together. Then his dream, his greatest desire, the fulfilment of his life, was threatened. His ultimate ambition was at risk. What hope did he have now?

For Mary had written that they should switch to Skype. She said she could not go on without him knowing what she looked like. Sharing their feelings had been paramount to their friendship. Now, she said, the time had come to reveal something they had not discussed.

David was distraught – for he had been blind from birth and hadn't told her. The girl for whom he yearned wanted to press a key that he thought might end everything he held most precious. He was sure that life would not be worth living without her. The apps on his computer that converted text to the spoken word and vice versa, the 'Audible Narration' for his Kindle books, and the keyboard that enabled him to earn his living (along with the computer that went with it) were his eyes on the world he could not see; all the apparatus that he had mastered, and upon which he was totally dependent, would be of little value without his precious Mary.

One of David's most valued possessions was his tactile world globe. It had been given to him a year earlier by an uncle who brought it back from America. This globe had been designed for the sight-impaired. It had raised markings on its surface annotated in Braille. Hardly a day passed when he did not feel his way around the world to where he knew the love of his life lived.

'God grant me the Serenity to accept the things I cannot change; Courage to change the things that I can; and the Wisdom to know the difference.' This famous prayer by Reinhold Niebuhr had inspired him for many years. He had acquired the serenity to accept his condition and shown immense courage through his determination and hard work. Today he was independent and able to support himself. Blindness was not a handicap. In his mind he was just a little different from most.

At seventeen years of age David had suffered a crushing blow when his parents were killed in a car crash. That tragedy gave witness to the strength of his character. At an early age he was taken in as a boarder at the RNIB (Royal National Institute for the Blind) College at Loughborough, UK. He was an only child, and had been living with his parents near Nottingham during the holidays. At Loughborough he had flourished, and developed his skills – the skills that he practised as a training officer for the blind and partially sighted.

David, now twenty-two years of age, had an apartment in an extra-care sheltered-housing scheme. He knew he was luckier than most in that he had a tenancy for life and help was on hand when he needed it, including meals in a community dining room which also provided him with the social contact that relieved the many hours he spent alone in his room at his computer. His initial reaction of hopelessness at Mary's latest suggestion turned to determination. He knew there was a wide belief that blind people could not live 'normal' lives. He was fearful of the view Mary's parents might take. She was nineteen and living at home with them. He could not bear the thought of losing the girl with whom he had fallen so deeply in love.

Life had taught him to think carefully as well as literally step warily before taking action of any sort. He needed more time to think. All was not lost – he knew there had to be a way.

He deliberately made no contact with her for a week, not replying to the emails which came from her every day, asking what was wrong. Then, for the first time, he sent her an outright lie.

'My darling Mary,' he emailed, 'I have been ill. Nothing for you to worry about. I am over the worst and staying with good friends who say I must rest. My doctor has told me not to return to work for a few weeks. Be in touch soon. I love you more each day and yearn to be with you – David.'

Mary knew how David also loved his work. He had written of the computer technology and other skills he taught to people with different and varied impairments. Indeed it was David who had inspired her to study computer programming and it was Internet social media that had brought them together in the first instance. Now she replied, saying how she longed to be with him, to hold him, to help him recover and get back to work. She still did not tell him the one thing about herself that she had held back since their first online encounter. Her parents knew she hadn't told him. What they also knew was that if David was half the man their daughter said he was, they must find a way to help her fulfil her right to happiness and achieve the one thing that mattered most in her life.

"Missy, my love," said her mother a couple of days after Mary had told her parents the latest news about David. "Your poppa and I have been talking. You have worked hard at your studies. What you need is a holiday – a break. You can take your laptop and keep in touch with David. Let's go pack your things. We're off tomorrow for a few days – and don't ask us where we are going."

Mary smiled and muttered her thanks.

When they arrived by taxi at Jackson Hole Airport, Wyoming, Mary's parents knew they could no longer keep their destination secret.

"We are not just taking you on a mystery holiday," said her mother; "we are taking you to England to meet the man in your life."

Her face broke into a smile, and then the tears began to flow.

"But I haven't told him . . ." And her voice trailed away. "I was going to, but something always stopped me. It didn't seem that important," she sobbed. "We can't go – we can't go."

"Yes we can," said her father. "If he's half the man we

all believe him to be it won't make any difference. We are not going to be around for ever, my darling Mary. We are not young any more. Parents have an instinct. Your mama and I have talked this over. We will never forgive ourselves if we don't give you this chance. Please, we beg you . . ."

The best that Virgin Airways could offer them on that long journey did little to dismiss the hidden anxiety that hung over the three of them during the many airborne hours. The self-drive from London Airport to the Travelodge in Nottingham was only slightly less tedious. Thus it was that on the third day since they had left home they drove to the address Mary had been given by David when they mailed each other Christmas presents last year. That address had not shown, by its nature, any clue that it was not a normal private residential dwelling.

The tasteful black noticeboard at the entrance to a short drive announced, in gold lettering, 'Burlington Court'. They came to an immaculate lawn the size of a football pitch laid out with paths, flower beds and wooden benches, all surrounded by a low hedge. Outside the hedge was a gravel driveway on three sides separating it from a terrace of brick-built single-storey homes, each with a small, neat front garden incorporating a paved parking space. The black-numbered white front doors were sheltered by an oak-timbered and tiled weather porch.

"Somebody round here must know where his friends live if he's not back yet," announced Mary's dad as they parked outside number seven.

Mary swayed and they each took an arm and walked with her to the front door. Mary's steps faltered a little.

"You are not alone, my lovely daughter. Remember we who also love you are here," said her mother as she wrapped her arm around Mary's shoulders, kissing her cheek and holding her tight.

"I'll ring the bell," said her dad.

A noise from within sounded like a safety chain being removed from its clasp. The door opened inwards. There stood a fair-haired handsome clean-shaven young man wearing soft brown leather moccasins, blue jeans and a white short-sleeved T-shirt with 'David' blazoned across the chest. He stepped into the open doorway.

As his unseeing eyes stared beyond the three of them, he spoke: "I am David. What can I do for you?"

The silence seemed like minutes, but it was only seconds. Mary was struck dumb by the sound of his voice, which she had only heard a few times during their Christmas phone calls.

"David," she almost shouted, "it's really you!"

Her parents held back, and with her hands outstretched she fell into his all-embracing arms as she stepped forward.

"It's Mary," she cried. "My beloved David, please forgive me. I was going to tell you, but . . ."

"You're blind – you're blind! It had to be. I knew!" he exclaimed, as he enveloped her in a crushing hug. "My darling, darling Mary."

It really was minutes this time before the tears of all four of them were cleared sufficiently for the explanations to tumble out. But none were needed.

THERE'S NONE SO DEAF . . .
(or, The Debt Collector's Fantasy)

I have an honours degree in acoustics engineering certified by the Institute of Acoustics, which, upon my graduation many years ago at Solent University, Southampton, UK, presented to me the annual Young Persons Award for Innovation. My company now specialises in the manufacture of high-quality miniature components, which we sell worldwide to top-end producers of earbuds, hearing aids and aural entertainment devices.

I did not relish the thought of what I had to say that morning as I walked round the corner to one of my first customers, and also my geographically nearest.

In the twenty years that we have been doing business with SuperDooperAuraProducts (SDAP) Ltd it has changed ownership three times, but happily Bill Harbin, the original factory production manager, has stayed throughout. Nevertheless, this time I did not expect him to greet me like an old friend as always. But he did.

"Come in, Tom. Have a seat. To what do I owe this honour?"

I could see that he had no idea why I had called.

"Bill, old pal, I hope I do not have to deliver bad news for both of us. Can you please tell me why, despite repeated requests, we haven't been paid by your company for over three months?"

Bill's eyebrows nearly took off and then furrowed deeply.

"What!" he shouted. "You've got to be kidding me."

"How I wish that were true," I said sadly, and continued: "Despite several phoned requests and three letters – zilch. This visit, Bill, is to tell you that I am here today to collect what is owed to us or reluctantly cease deliveries."

"What!" shouted Bill again. "Our production line will come to a halt."

Breathing heavily Bill grabbed his phone, stabbed a few numbers and demanded to know from his accounts department what was going on. Whatever was said caused him to cut off and redial.

He addressed the person on the other end: "Sir," he growled, "I have an important supplier here in my office who tells me his company has not been paid for months."

He was drowned out before he could say any more as an irate male voice (I could hear it from the other side of the desk) shouted, "Send him up to me."

"How dare you discuss money matters with my production manager!" said the managing director the moment his secretary ushered me into his office. Before I could utter a single word, ignoring my outstretched hand, he announced, "If you have a complaint it is to me that such matters should be directed." I was not offered a seat and he remained in his own chair behind his desk. "What did you say your name was? What is the name of your company?"

"My name is Tom Gatrall, sir, and my company is AudioGatrall Ltd," I said politely, having waited over half an hour outside his office before he deigned to see me.

I explained about the phone calls and letters asking for payment of our account, which was now four months overdue. I told him that we were still prepared to continue supplying his company under certain conditions. I reminded him that we had solved a technical problem for them many years ago that no other company apparently could. I told him my condition was that the outstanding account of £325,492 must be settled with a banker's draft or building-society cheque today. Those of you familiar with bounced cheques will know that a banker's draft or a building-society cheque is as good as cash. I also explained that I required his guarantee that in future the account would be settled monthly. By the look of him I thought he was going to explode.

"AudioGatrall?" he practically shouted. "What exactly is it that you do?"

"Well, sir," I said, spotting a set of lightweight earbuds on his desk that his company manufactured, "if you would hand me those earpieces I will show you."

To my surprise he did as I asked, but not without opening his mouth again: "I hope you are not going to waste much more of my time," he said irritably.

I took the earpieces from him, unscrewed the outer cup from the left unit and removed a tiny diode (just 3 × 5 × 1.5 mm) with the small tweezers that I always carry with me. I screwed the cup on again and handed the set back to him.

"Without this component, which we supply, you will find the unit cannot produce clear sound. We make those mini semiconductors, which are patented to my company."

"Oh yes" was his sarcastic reply.

I had of course been trying to emphasise how important we were to him, fully aware that none of us are indispensable.

Next, he put his earpieces on and plugged them into a

little box on his desk, pressed a button and appeared to be listening intensely.

"This is our test unit," he said. "It plays sounds that cover the full range of frequencies that can be heard by the human ear. What I hear sounds no different to me without the bit that you have just removed. I think you should leave my office now and not waste any more of my time."

"Please, sir," I said, knowing that what he'd said could not be true, "that test equipment of yours is fascinating. May I just have a listen myself?"

He surprised me once again by handing the earpieces to me and pressing the button. It was at that point that I remembered what his production manager had told me, almost as a joke, many months ago: his new boss was deaf in one ear. I was about to suggest that he swopped the earpieces around on his head, but as soon as I opened my mouth to speak and offered the equipment back to him he snatched it from my hand, stood up, strode toward the door and held it open. I judged that his ignorance and arrogance really would have caused him to explode and have me thrown off the premises.

I did manage to get one sentence out as I turned to leave the room: "And what about the payment of my company's account, sir?"

He slammed the office door in my face.

And so I returned to my factory empty-handed. When all the guys had gone home I took apart the set of earbuds that my customer's friendly production manager had given me sometime ago as a present in recognition of the vital service that we had given. It took me just over ten minutes to modify the crossover network and then to type a letter addressed to my very rude customer.

PRIVATE AND CONFIDENTIAL

Dear Sir,

We have made the technical changes to our product which you insisted were required when I called today to ask you to settle our account. I enclose the modified set of earpieces for you to personally test to your satisfaction. Please note that we have not been able to carry out within the timetable you demanded the exhaustive tests in our laboratory for the changes in the production of certain harmonics and volume factors which I advised were absolutely essential for safety reasons prior to the general use of these buds.

Yours sincerely,

Tom Gatrall, Managing Director.

Next day, before instructing our solicitors to recover the debt, and reconciled to the fact that we had lost that particular customer, I gave the earpieces to old Mary Goodlove, who had for years not only looked after my mother before she died, but had unstintingly devoted herself since the day the company started to the very important task of leading a team cleaning our premises. By pure coincidence she also cleaned the offices of this very rude ex-customer just down the road after their staff had gone home for the day.

She dutifully swopped the earbuds I gave her with those on the managing director's desk and slipped my letter under a pile of papers in a tray on the same desk as I had asked her to. A few days later, after the security man who let her out of the building every night had informed her that the boss had reported sick and gone deaf in the other ear, she swopped the earpieces back again.

I think I should tell you that I won that award for innovation all those years back for a paper on NIHL (noise-induced hearing loss), which expounded on the possible dangers of the use of miniature capacitors in earbuds, headphones and hearing aids, which, if wired in a certain way, could produce a noise as loud as a gunshot – maybe up to 190 decibels. Such an event so close to the tympanic membrane would have a devastating effect on the wearer. I promised at the time not to reveal details of my findings in case they were used vindictively. I never did, and never will. I did, however, write one more letter to my very rude and ignorant customer.

Dear Sir,

Thank you for the belated payment of arrears to my company. This is to assure you that you will not be hearing from us further.

Yours most sincerely,

Tom Gatrall, Managing Director.

SPECIAL DELIVERY

"No! You bloody well listen to me Fred – you've worked your backside off all your stinking life getting me put away. What makes you think I can bloody well trust you now after all these bucking years?"

"Doug, please, just control that foul mouth of yours for a few minutes. I'll give you credit for being a smart operator. You are not stupid. Now just keep your gob shut and lend me your ears long enough for you to hear an offer you cannot refuse. You are fifty-four years old, but you look more like 100 after all those beatings-up from your so-called mates. You have an incurable cancer. Here we are offering to help. Now listen to me."

Doug fell silent. He was not called Doug the Drug for no good reason; nor had he spent most of his life in prison for no good reason. But there was a good reason for making him an unprecedented offer. Doug had served ten sentences, totalling thirty-two years, as a guest of Her Majesty's Prison Service.

One day a practical-thinking member of the Advisory Council to the Prison Service persuaded the authorities that as Doug had already cost the country over a million pounds, and knew more about the drugs problem in prisons than all of the advisors put together, it was time to realise that it would make more sense to bring him onside rather than to treat him as the enemy. His value to the state could be moved from negative to positive at no extra cost.

Fred was known to the underground world as Fred the Filth. His real identity was kept secret by the authorities. Even the Home Secretary was not allowed to know the name of the drug squad's oldest and most favoured and successful operator.

"You and I both know that you do not have much more time on this earth," continued Fred. "We also know that you have more enemies than friends, most of whom would like to see you under the turf. The powers that be have decided that you may live out the rest of your life in a place where you will receive the best possible medical treatment and be safe from the murderous villains you have cheated and deceived over many years and who would also like nothing better than to stick a knife into your stinking rotten guts."

"No such bleeding secure place exists" was Doug the Drug's vehement response.

"Wrong" was Fred's reply. "You will be in a nursing home – a place where security is as good as any prison and the occupants are not a bunch of murderous low-down scum such as you have been living with all your life. You will have a new identity. The residents are checked every twenty minutes. You will have an en-suite room, a balcony overlooking the countryside and all meals provided. Your comfort and well-being will be far superior to anything you could ever have dreamed about."

"I'll believe it when I bloody see it," replied Doug.

A week later Fred watched Doug like a hawk whilst he was packing his grubby bags. Fred then drove him from the shabby flat in London's East End to the nursing home out in the countryside, where his future life of comparative luxury had been arranged.

On arrival, Fred introduced him to the staff as his son, Douglas Foster. This private home had previously been required to understand that the £70,000-per-annum rate of care being funded by his father came with strict instructions that he should have no visitors or phone calls at any time without his dad's express permission and that any letters or packages addressed to him would be first inspected by his dad, who was contactable at any time of the day or night. Reception was manned from 8 a.m. to 5 p.m. Doors from there into the residents' areas had coded access locks. All doors to the outside were kept permanently locked for the security of residents and staff alike.

"Bloody marvellous!" exclaimed Doug as he and Fred surveyed his accommodation on that first day.

Fred went over the house rules, which he had drawn up and which Doug then signed. He could ask the staff for his dad any time. No other contact with the outside world was permitted. In return Doug was required, in the parlance of common criminals, to sing like a canary.

Bear with me, dear readers, and you will see how particularly apposite this phrase actually is.

However, being banned from fraternising with other residents resulted in Doug becoming lonely. In the past even sitting on the loo was usually in the company of at least one other crook. Additionally, despite the double glazing, from 7 a.m. until 11 p.m. the noise of aircraft taking off from the west end of the airport runway a couple of miles away was occasionally still intrusive to residents on the top floor, one of whom was Doug. So Doug set about applying his fertile and totally corrupt mind to turning this problem to his advantage.

It had occurred to the staff that Fred Foster didn't look anything like his dad, but it was not part of their remit to check the information they had been given. What was part of their remit, however, was to take blood or urine tests from residents who indicated psychotic symptoms. Our man often did, and always refused such attention – which was his right, of course.

Doug had regular visits from his dad, who brought all sorts of goodies, including his favourite packets of jelly beans. Meetings with 'Dad' in the privacy of his room were proving invaluable to the authorities. His willingness to 'sing' had something to do with their threat to reveal his location if he didn't. He had a large metal cash box with a combination lock, in which, he told Fred, he would keep notes as they came to mind about the villains that the authorities wanted to know about.

"The few personal memories I have left!" he would say to the staff as he wiped away a tear; and they would smile kindly as he hid the contents of this large box from their view.

No one questioned why Doug kept his treasured old fishing rod in the corner of his room; nor did they know that he had never caught a fish in his whole life. Neither did Fred know at first that Doug had managed to smuggle in his mobile phone, which he kept in his cash box. When Fred did find out he did not tell Doug, but secretly installed a microphone in Doug's room to find out what was going on. Now he knew. He discovered that the fertile mind to which I referred earlier had indeed enabled Doug to ingeniously take advantage of the aircraft distraction.

Before Fred had found out about the mobile Doug had recruited an old lag known as Charley the Chopper. This crook, as his name implied, was a drone expert. He had been supplying Doug with his happy pills (known in prisons as Spice, or to the enlightened as synthetic cannabinoids). By means of Doug's mobile they would arrange a time during darkness, but before flying ceased at 11 p.m., when the noise of a scheduled airliner on its climb out from the nearby airport was at its loudest. Charley would launch his electric 'quadcopter' drone from the field behind the home.

Charley used autonomy technology to fly it to a predetermined point above the home, where it hovered so that the 'supplies', in the form of what looked like a 160-gram packet of jelly beans hung down outside Doug's balcony on the end of a weighted fifty-foot plumb line. Lit by the lights from the room, Doug caught the line with his fishing rod, unhooked the bag and replaced it with another bag containing a numbered key and instructions as where to find a safe-deposit box that contained £5,000 in cash. Under cover of the noise from the climbing jet, Charley retrieved his battery-powered drone.

This use of technology had previously enabled the two of them to fool one prison authority close to another noisy airport many times. The operation took just under two minutes.

Doug had chosen an empty sweet bag with its convenient hole in the package name card (designed to hang on hooks in shops) to smuggle his 'sweeties' in, as well as to send back to Charley not only one key at a time, but also an address and the essential password for the lock it fitted out of the hundreds of safe-deposit boxes, each containing five grand, that he had, over thirty years during his rare days of freedom, prepaid and long-term-rented all over London. This arrangement, he explained to Charlie, was called 'cash on delivery'.

Then one day came trouble. There was no bag on the end of the hook when Charley retrieved his machine after the delivery. No bag meant no key and no cash. Charley called Doug on his mobile immediately.

"I know what you're up to, Doug. You're not bloody well going to get away with your usual dirty tricks – not on me you ain't. I want two keys in future or I'll get up to me own tricks, which you won't like a bit, me old mate. So, remember, two keys for the last lot, and in future the price 'as gorn up by one 'undred per cent. That makes two keys every time – gorit?"

"Double be damned. Don't be bleeding greedy" was all Doug was able to say before Charley cut him off.

Now, what you didn't know was that Doug had a canary in his room. He had always had a pet canary and Fred had seen no harm in him continuing to have one. Doug, however, likened it to the canaries that coal miners used to take down into the pits to detect carbon monoxide. Over the years Doug had unhappily lost several canaries before he had finally found the correct dose that wouldn't kill the bird – it just fell off its perch if the stuff was safe.

Knowing some of the nasty habits of the unsavoury characters supplying him, Doug had perfected his method of testing the potency of his happy pills. He would dissolve half a pill into the bird's drinking water.

If it was still alive an hour after falling off its perch, and merely staggering around at the bottom of the cage, he judged the batch to be safe.

Shortly after the next delivery the canary died. You'd think that Doug would heed a warning, but not a bit of it – he still put only one key in the return bag with the instructions as to where to collect the money. Nobody except Doug's dad connected the explosion that occurred when someone tried to open a safe-deposit box in Paddington with a canary that had died in a nursing home thirty miles to the west.

During Charley's stay in hospital they repaired his face as best they could. They also managed to save his eyesight and told him he was lucky to be alive. Doug's fertile mind, to which we have previously drawn attention, had ensured that he had built up a surplus of 'sweeties' that could keep him going for quite some time in the event of unforeseen problems. Thus the weight of his cash box hadn't altered much as his hoard of pills replaced the weight of the keys that had left it.

Before Christmas Doug asked his dad if he could break the rule of having to stay in his room. He was allowed to join the others in the dining room just for the festive lunch on Christmas Day. Forty or so old folks wearing paper hats and fortified with rum punch, served before the meal and wine with it, were sat around the tables. Some regular carers and a number of volunteers from outside were helping to make this a joyous occasion for the residents. One of these volunteers, in a Father Christmas outfit, with a huge white beard and moustache, kept topping up Doug's glass.

When Doug was showing obvious signs of inebriation this helper whispered to a busy carer, "The old boy's 'ad a little too much. He's asked me to 'elp him up to his room. We'll be fine."

When they were alone in Doug's room Charley spoke again: "Didn't recognise me, Doug, did you?" he said rather loudly. Without waiting for an answer he continued: "For fifty grand I'll give you the antidote."

Charley was now alone with Doug in his room. He explained to him how he had doped his wine. For a week, he told Doug, he would suffer dizziness, anxiety and hallucinations. In the second week he would advance to vomiting and seizures. Then paralysis would set in, and by the end of January he would suffer a most painful death. The antidote had to be taken in two doses – one now and the other a week later. Charley also thought it reasonable to ask his friend for half the ransom now in the form of five keys and the necessary information, in return for which he would give him the first dose right away. Then he promised the second dose when he came back after the holiday to enquire how he was getting on after his 'overindulgence' at the Christmas party. And of course to collect the balance of his blackmail – i.e. another five keys.

"How do I know you'll come back, you bastard?" slurred Doug as he slumped on to the bed.

"I expected you to ask that," said Charley as he reached into his jacket and produced a fancy stainless-steel box the size of and looking like a cigar case with a five-number combination lock. "You select ten keys that open your cash-filled deposit boxes now. I will shuffle them and give you five back in this little box. Then you give me the addresses and password information for all ten. The code for this box is only known to me. You can keep it until I come back again for the other five next week. So that guarantees I will be back. It would be exceedingly stupid of you to select any key now that might lead me again into one of your death traps or to a box with no bleeding cash. Unless of course you fancy a very unpleasant death."

Suddenly they were interrupted by a knock on the door as a carer entered.

"Shno problem, my dear," said Doug. "Turns out thish man and I were in the shame trade; we've been chatting. I jusht overdid it a bit. Going to resht for a few minutes."

Charley left with the five keys and instructions.

A week later Charley turned up at the home again, this time with another false beard. When he asked after Doug's health he was told to wait as the old boy had been very unwell ever since Christmas. After half an hour or so Fred arrived at the home, went straight up to Charley and showed him his warrant card. Charley paled at the thought of becoming a guest yet again of Her Majesty's Prison Service, but Fred just smiled.

"I know why you're here, Charley. Come with me," said Fred, and he steered Charley upstairs to Doug's room. Doug was lying in bed when they walked into his room without knocking.

"Before you two start trying to kill each other again," said Fred, "I would like you both to know that I am here on the friendliest of missions. I have informed the home manager that I am going to allow you, Charley, to visit Doug any time. I really think now that he should have a friend to visit as well as myself."

Doug and Charley eyed each other without saying a word.

Fred continued: "I will explain. As Doug well knows, I am an officer with Her Majesty's Investigations & Intelligence Service, Drug Squad Branch. After serious consideration we have decided to offer you, Charley, the same deal that Doug enjoys and which I will now explain to you. We are aware of what you two have been up to. Such behaviour doesn't suit the best interests of any of us. Your decision, Charley, to accept our offer will be made more easy, we suspect, if I tell you that you will be on a murder charge should Doug succumb to the poison you have fed him or should he come to harm at any time in the future." Fred explained to Charley the deal on offer and the house rules he would have to sign.

Charley, without saying a word, produced a little bottle and handed it to Doug, who, also without speaking, unscrewed the stopper and swallowed the contents.

"He will live," declared Charley. "In a few days he'll be fine, but you must agree that Doug will live a little longer if you give me time to organise a future supply of his special sweeties and put it about to the effing underworld about my impending trip to the farthest distant wilds of the earth. Also," continued Charley, "in about a month I will have grown a real beard. My face is badly disfigured and none of my contacts in the underworld have seen me since or even know about the accident that caused it. I will also need to leave this excellent establishment from time to time, not only to collect Doug's 'supplies', but, more importantly for you, so that I can keep up to date with what's going on and provide you with the very latest information – for which you are paying most 'an'somely, I might say."

Fred wrote by hand into the typed official document he had brought with him the amendments Charley had suggested, insisting that, once installed, in a month's time he must return to the home every evening and clock in by 5 p.m. Fred also told Charley that he would be given a new name, that he must advise him every time he left the home and when he had returned, and that he would receive anonymity only if he behaved himself. If he didn't they would reveal him as a snitch and leave him to his fate.

Charley signed.

Fred wagged his finger vigorously. "Remember this, you two piles of crap. You keep to your sides of the agreement and we'll keep to ours and look after you. But we won't shed a single tear if either of you finish up under the turf as a result of double-crossing us like you have your mates over the years."

As soon as they were alone and certain Fred had left the building Doug looked at Charley and held his forefinger to his lips. He stood on a chair, removed a microphone hidden in the ceiling light fitting and stamped on it.

"It bloody worked!" he cried. "But the filth will be round in the morning for certain to find out what happened to their mike. I'll tell 'em I couldn't continue to do business with people I couldn't trust!"

The two of them became nearly paralytic with laughter.

"But truly, old pal," Doug continued with his arm round Charley's shoulders when they had recovered sufficiently to speak, "I am really sorry that you were hurt. I did instruct you in my note to stand well back, you stupid ass."

Charley turned to his old friend. "Well, it certainly

added authenticity to our story, didn't it? They were convinced I was out to do you in. They hadn't a clue that we knew they'd tapped into our conversations. With our new identities and me with a new face we can spend the rest of our lives in safety from all those crooks out there!"

The two of them again erupted into laughter.

"You're a bleeding genius, Doug, me old mate, for thinking this one up."

"And you, you old sod," chuckled Doug, "will show your gratitude by coming and going incognito with my favourite sweeties."

On Doug's fifty-fifth birthday a couple of months later he had a party in his room. The only guests were his 'new' bearded friend, who had been busy shopping that morning and arrived with lobster, champagne and other goodies, and his dad. Because of the pressure of work Fred had to get back to head office after an hour or so, leaving the two old lags to their own devices.

On the way out Fred confirmed to the management that John Smith, Doug's new friend and recently arrived resident in their 'care without nursing facilities' in the next-door building, could be trusted to honour his strict instructions concerning no other visitors to his son and the receipt of parcels, etc. He was convinced, he told them, that visits to Doug by John in addition to himself would be beneficial. He did not explain to whom else it would be beneficial or why.

THE TREE

The four-foot wall of the ha-ha faced away from the end of John's tiny back garden, giving a clear view over it from his living room down to the village in the valley below. That and the low drystone walls at the sides were all that separated his property from the livestock in the steep fields around. Fields too steep and too rich in clay for the plough, but ideal for grass and the hardy Cheviot sheep that were now grazing the meadows. Meadows that had been a blaze of wildflowers when the agent introduced him to the cottage some months previously.

"People don't even lock their doors round these parts," the estate agent had said as John signed the papers on the old kitchen table. "This is England as it used to be."

Now at last John had found the peace and quiet he'd planned for years. Years of planning that nearly went wrong, he was thinking. He would take his time to replace the shabby old furniture which had been included in the modest price he had paid for this little old cottage. He owned nothing of his own to install and looked forward to the redecorating and modernising which he would do himself. A new life. There was no hurry.

"Time to live again," he said to himself as he exited his back door and closed the gate into the lane at the side. He had been confined, and now the open spaces called. This is what he'd longed for – fresh air, grass, trees, flowers, birdsong and isolation. The smell of the countryside hung in the still of a windless afternoon; the bees hovered about their business in the late summer floral offerings. No more the foul odour of unwashed human bodies, no more the cacophony of an overcrowded city. He had his very own lane. It terminated at his cottage – just a cart track really, which led to one end of the village High Street. It meandered down the hill past wide gates that led into grassy fields on either side.

This afternoon he headed down that lane to explore the pub in the village below. As he walked he carefully rehearsed in his head what he would say to the first person he met. Since he had moved in a week earlier he had neither seen nor spoken to a soul. He surely would soon. He did – sooner than he expected – for just into a field, beyond an open barred gate, he saw a magnificent old oak tree. Like a giant green posy, as tall and as big as a house, with a trunk so massive that in all probability, he guessed, three people with arms outstretched could not encompass it. The lower branches were barely above head height. There, sitting on the ground in the shade among the gnarled roots with his back against the grey vertical ridges of the ancient bark, was a strange-looking figure.

This man sported a bushy white beard and a droopy moustache, and from beneath a shock of white hair peered tired blue eyes, sunk into their sockets and shielded by thick grey eyebrows. He was old in appearance, yet his skin was young and unwrinkled. His faded apparel was akin to those paintings of shepherds in olden times: a white cotton smock decorated with stitching, knee breeches, gaiters and boots. He was tossing acorns into a battered old tweed cap on the ground about six feet in front of him. As John watched from the gate unnoticed, every acorn the old man picked up from a pile beside him landed in his cap.

"Hello. I'm new around these parts. My name is John," he said as he entered the field and approached across the grass.

The man did not answer, just picked up another acorn and tossed it into his cap.

"You're pretty good at that," continued John.

The man slowly looked up, his face expressionless, and with a nod of acknowledgement returned his gaze to his cap and then spoke just a few words quietly in a gentle West Country accent: "I be the champion in days gone by, 'till they done for me."

John waited for more words, but none came. Not wishing to be intrusive, he turned to leave.

"I'll be off, then," he said to the old man. "I've moved into the cottage just up the lane. Come and see me any time."

There was no further response.

John retraced his steps to the gate and, with a wave of his hand, continued down the lane.

The pub was where he remembered it when he first came searching for his hideaway – just outside the village. Nothing fancy – not a tourist Mecca. It looked as if it had once been a row of farmworkers' cottages. It was brick-built, with a thatched roof and three little thatched upper-floor dormer windows. Tubs of bright flowers and heavy wooden picnic tables were outside on the wide paved area adjacent to the road.

Inside, the white ceiling was low; all around were dark varnished high-backed benches softened with comfortable emerald-green fitted cushions. In front of them there were scrubbed oak tables on a stone-flagged floor, all surrounded by beechwood panelled walls. There was a shove-ha'penny board at the end of one of the long tables.

"My name is John," he said for the second time that afternoon to only the second person he'd spoken to that day, as he approached the man sitting on a high stool behind the bar reading a newspaper. "I seem to be the first one in this evening."

"Ah! I'm Tom, the landlord" was the reply. "'Tis normally quiet this early of a Monday. Now, what can I do for you?"

"I'm new around here. Name's John. Just moved in up the road. You wouldn't by any chance have a local ale that you could recommend?"

"Indeed we have, sir, Royal Oak. Pint or half?"

Over the next hour or two they had few interruptions as the landlord related a grisly story. Several pints of Royal Oak had slipped down their throats by the time Tom concluded.

"Some do say it's a myth, but I'm inclined to think it's true." Tom held on to the counter with one hand for support as he rocked on his stool. "Anyway, who would make up such a story, eh?"

"You would," said John with a laugh that covered his concern, for he had become increasingly troubled as Tom's story evolved. "I've really enjoyed thish evening, but it'll be dark before I can find my way home! There'sh no street lights up that old lane. Musht be off." He picked up his change from the bar and lurched toward the door. "She you shoon, Tom."

As John started on his way home he recalled the

landlord's story, which dated back some 100 years or so. All the land around for miles was owned at that time by the squire who lived in the manor house at the other end of the village. Home Farm surrounded the village – and yes, as John had surmised, the pub had indeed been a terrace of three cottages that housed farmworkers. In one of these lived a young shepherd with his parents. Most of the farm's livestock were sheep.

This young man, so rumour went, had raped the squire's fifteen-year-old daughter. It was said that the daughter become pregnant as a result. The young girl was the squire's only child, whose mother had died during her birth. She was brought up by her father and his housekeeper – the only occupants of the manor house. Not much was heard of this young girl after the alleged rape until the announcement of her death. Rumour was that she too, like her mother, had died in childbirth. The baby was stillborn, and with her dying words the young girl was supposed to have whispered the name of the baby's father, a farmworker, to the squire's housekeeper.

The young shepherd in question had been in the habit of climbing oak trees to collect acorns prior to the annual village fair, where in those days there was a booth at which one could purchase twelve acorns for a penny. If, standing on a small mat, the contestant managed to toss all twelve acorns into a jar a few feet away they could win a shilling. This young man apparently spent hours practising, and thus was a regular winner.

Early one morning soon after the death of the squire's daughter became known – though not the cause – this lad was found hanging from a branch of an oak tree. The magistrates decided that the rope he used to climb trees in order to collect his acorns had somehow got tangled round his neck when he fell. His parents got permission from the squire to bury him under the tree where he was found.

In his will the squire had stipulated that when the three cottages which he owned at the end of the High Street became vacant his estate should provide so that they could be converted into a tavern to be named The Tree, '*where suitable refreshment can be obtained, and provision shall be made therein for a room where matters of import to residents of the village may be examined. This room is to be named The Oak Room.*'

"So here it stands to this day," Tom had said, unsteady on his stool and waving his arm around as he pointed to a room that led off from the bar. "The original wooden hand-painted pub sign of an old oak tree is still outside, it was suspended from a gibbet on two thick ropes. The gibbet is still there, but the ropes ain't rope no more – 'ealth and safety, you understand. Them ropes were said to have been cut from the one that hanged that poor lad. Oh!" Tom had added, "I near forgot – the squire 'imself died just a month after they buried the lad. Fallen off his horse an' all while out visiting his tenant farmers. Broke his neck. Apparently this surprised the locals for he was a youngish man, an accomplished horseman and master of the local hunt. Found by his housekeeper, they do say. She is said to have gone looking for him when he failed to return for his supper. She evidently was an aunt of the young shepherd lad and indeed a most handsome spinster, by all accounts."

Tom had finished his story by telling John that after the squire's funeral the housekeeper moved out from the manor house into Beech Cottage up the hill, which was another provision revealed in the squire's will. "There she lived out a reclusive and comfortable life, rent-free, and talking to very few. Following the death of the young shepherd she was reported to have told someone that the evening before the lad was found hanging she had seen the squire up near the field where the poor chap succumbed. Religious sort of woman she was," Tom had said. And then added, "Strange thing is that nobody's ever lived for very long in that same old cottage at the top of the lane."

Staggering up the hill, anxious that what was bothering him should only be to do with too much ale, John looked for the oak tree and the man in the field that he had spoken to on the way down. It was getting dark. He found the field, but could see no more than the silhouette of that giant oak tree against the darkening blue sky of nightfall. He did not fancy going into that field to investigate further.

The brightest stars were already visible as he zigzagged up the hill between the hedgerows. Twice he stumbled over the grass-covered central ridge of the steep lane. He began to curse that he had chosen such a place.

When they found his body a week later it was seated in a wooden chair hunched over the kitchen table, on which was a copy of the *Straits Times*, Singapore. It was open at a page whose headline pronounced, 'Englishman Found Not Guilty of Murdering Wife'.

The article went on to say that John Brown, an Englishman described as an import/export agent, having spent five years in Changi Prison after being found guilty of murdering his wealthy Chinese wife, had been freed by the Court of Appeal on the grounds of 'insufficient evidence'. The fact that was instrumental in getting him convicted in the original trial was that shortly before the murder he had been made bankrupt and stood to inherit a fortune from his wife's will.

At his first trial his defence was that he had been out jogging at the time of his wife's death – something he had done every night between 10 p.m. and midnight for years prior to the break-in. He had called the police, he said, when on returning home one night he found his wife bound and gagged and their apartment ransacked. The plaster stuck over her face had made it impossible for her to breathe – thus she had been asphyxiated. On his release after the appeal John Brown left the country.

The inquest on John Smith of Beech Cottage returned a finding that he had choked on his own vomit. No relatives could be traced. He died intestate with a very large sum of Singapore dollars deposited in a Swiss bank. What nobody seemed to have noticed, when Beech Cottage was searched for clues as to whether John Smith's death might be anything other than the misadventure verdict finally reached, was either the very old and faded framed tapestry on the kitchen wall that proclaimed 'Be ye sure your sins will find you out' or the acorn that had been crushed underfoot beside the unlocked back door.

OUR PLACE

OUR PLACE

I want you to know that the title above had a very special meaning for those of us who used to live in our quiet little village south of London, England, during the Second World War.

In this place we talked, we sang, we danced, we ate, we played, we prayed. I was one of nearly 200 who kneeled here one morning in the spring of 1945 and prayed for peace and deliverance from evil. The prayers were led by our priest, whose church and the adjacent vicarage had just suffered a direct hit from one of the last Nazi V-2 rockets fired across the Channel at Great Britain.

On the day the rocket fell – as usual with no warning, for being supersonic one heard the whoosh of its arrival after the explosion – our priest was visiting a sick parishioner at the far end of the village.

At Our Place ten days later I was privileged to read the prayer for our brave vicar. Brave because he led the Sunday prayers for which we were gathered that morning immediately after we had laid to rest his wife and baby son in the debris-littered churchyard nearby.

Carved into a solid piece of oak above the rusting corrugated-iron doors of the place where we prayed were the words 'Our Place'. In those days to say "See you at Our Place" was never misunderstood by any of the locals. Not grand enough to be called the village hall, we youngsters irreverently called it the Tin Hut. This little white painted building, standing in its own ground at the end of the High Street had been owned by the villagers for as long as anyone could remember. Furnished with wooden folding chairs, trestle tables and an old wood-fired kitchen range plus a small stage at the far end it had hosted a huge variety of celebrations from twenty-first birthday parties to Scout meetings and the British Legion.

The post-war years passed, the church and the vicarage were rebuilt, but the wooden structure with the corrugated-iron walls and roof no longer met the health-and-safety standards that regulations required and that people demanded.

Parishioners prefer posher places for their parties. The vicar has now joined his family in the churchyard. Sometimes visitors, sitting on the fine oak bench in the memorial garden that we built on the site of the old Tin Hut, not knowing who were 'Elizabeth and Baby Jamie', named on the little brass plate behind them, also wonder at the origin of that piece of weathered oak mounted on a post at the entrance to the garden. On it are carved two barely legible words. But I'll wager that today all those living in the village know exactly where to go when they are invited by one another to meet at Our Place.

ROBBERY?

I was intrigued when, after over thirty years, I received a phone call from an old university pal to meet him in a pub in Soho, London. After a good laugh about barely recognising each other, Harry Naughton wouldn't let me get a word in edgeways from the moment we sat down with our beers.

Harry told me about his new dental surgery. He told me how, as he approached retirement, he'd decided to set up on his own at home. He had converted the downstairs front half of his house into a surgery, complete with waiting room/reception and a lavatory. He'd also had a very large extension built at the back of the house big enough to be called a ballroom with a square of parquet flooring in the middle of a carpeted area, a long bar down one side and a raised platform at one end complete with grand piano. A conservatory-type domed glass roof with a crystal chandelier in the middle completed the extravagant decor.

This room was adjacent to the old lounge, which joined up with their private living space, including an enlarged kitchen, utility room, additional lavatory and the stairway to the bedrooms upstairs. There was a separate entrance to all this domestic accommodation and the bedrooms upstairs from the passage at one side of the house.

Their large mock-Tudor residence, he told me, was in the heart of Hampstead's most upmarket residential area. Harry went on to explain that it had taken years of networking and hefty legal expenses to finalise the planning consent. I was beginning to wonder why he had indicated in his phone call that it was so urgent for us to meet again.

"But why on earth do you want a ballroom, for goodness' sake?" I interrupted. "If my memory serves me right you couldn't dance a step."

"Good grief, Fred! I've only seen you a couple of times since we were both students at the Dental Institute, King's College, together, and that was nearly forty years ago. Things change, you know. . . . and anyway, you've never met my wife."

"Sorry, old pal – I guess we've a lot of catching up to do. . . . have another pint?"

"Now, that's more how I remember it. Let me give you some history. I didn't dig you out again without a very good reason."

Harry went on to tell me that early in his dental career he had married his then wealthiest client, Monique de Montfort. She was an elegant woman, not so much known for her intellect, but more for her riches, who was always to be seen literally dripping in diamonds and precious metal. She could best be described as a socialite. Her father, Rudolph de Montfort, had been a diamond merchant in Hatton Garden. Her mother, like her father, was descended from Hungarian nobility. Both her parents had died over twenty years ago. She was an only child and her inheritance had been considerable.

"Please hear me out, Fred. You not only have the skills that I need, but you are also the only person I can trust. At King's we developed a rapport. Remember how we discussed at length what we wanted out of life and how we were going to get it?"

"I do indeed," I replied. "Like all students, we spent hours dreaming and discussing how we were going to become rich. Sounds like you've achieved your ambition. How can I possibly help? You know I'm no longer in the dentistry business. Haven't been for over twenty years."

"I'm coming to that, Fred. Please stick with me a little longer, and after another pint all will be revealed. I used to beg Monique not to wear her valuable jewels, which hung from her ears, formed chains round her neck, adorned massive silver brooches and bracelets, and were set into gold rings on every finger. I used to wonder sometimes how she could bear the weight of all that stuff."

Over yet another pint I went on to learn from Harry that the Hampstead house was centred in half an acre, surrounded with mature eight-foot-tall dense Leylandii evergreen hedges. A short, broad gravel drive widened out into a space at the front of the house, which was now the entrance to the surgery, and big enough to park seven or eight cars. It was protected by CCTV and the latest intruder deterrents, but what had been worrying Harry was that there was no way that he could protect his wife. They had no children, which left her free to practise a lifestyle which he said was once described by *The Guardian* as 'vulgar'.

The conditions of the company which insured her jewellery (last valued at £28 million) stipulated that it would not be covered for loss when taken or worn outside the confines of their house and garden, and even then it was insured only when she was either wearing it or when it was locked in their private safe. Hence the ballroom, where Harry reckoned she could entertain her idle friends and remain covered by the risk of loss. The occasions when some of her personal adornments were not insured were unfortunately frequent as she travelled alone around the world, spending most of Harry's hard-earned but not inconsiderable income and overtly displaying her wealth.

"You and I, Fred, worked our backsides off to get our degrees at King's. I stuck to our profession and eventually became a partner in the Mayfair dental practice, which I joined straight from university. You on the other hand packed it in early in your career, went into the jewellery business and I haven't heard from you for years. Then I read about you in the newspapers recently, remembered our friendship and an idea came into my head."

"I take it you are referring to the robbery that took place at the Tower of London?"

Harry's reply was a nod of his head, a raising of eyebrows and a purposeful grin. Without further comment on what had been an incident in my life that had considerably boosted my retirement plans, Harry went on to tell me that Monique's capacity for extravagance was exceeding their income. This had not unduly worried him at first because, as a result of the valuation of her jewellery, he imagined they could both live comfortably in their old age on the proceeds of its sale at auction when the time came. However, there was a snag or two.

Snag number one was that she had sworn many times that she would never stoop so low as to sell one single item of her family heirlooms. Another factor that had to be taken into account was that many of her friends lived locally, sought expensive dental procedures, and had become some of Harry's most profitable and essential patients. I got the impression that his wife's friends were more important to him than she was herself.

What worried Harry most, however, he said, was that his wife was an easy target when outside the house for kidnappers, blackmailers or worse. In addition, she was now being paid excessive attention by the handsome young piano player that she regularly hired for her monthly soirées in the ballroom. Harry then confided to me that Monique was fifteen years younger than himself and that he was, as I knew, like myself, approaching sixty-five and looking for a comfortable retirement.

"Fred, old pal," he said, standing up to leave, "I have a plan which I believe will solve my problems and at the same time make us both very wealthy. You are the only person with the skills needed, and in whom I can trust. Will you help me?"

"Of course, of course," I answered, "provided it is legal."

It was another six months before I heard again from Harry.

* * * * * * * * *

"Fred," said the voice on the other end of the phone, "remember our meeting in Soho? Well, the time has arrived for action. Can you come over, please? It's urgent."

What follows is what he told me later that day over dinner in his kitchen. Monique was out for the evening. He seemed keen that I should leave before she returned.

Apparently, at about midnight in the middle of Monique's fiftieth birthday extravaganza the previous week, all the lights in the house went out. Amidst the pandemonium and flashing of a few of the guests' smartphone lights and torches he urged people in the ballroom to sit quietly in a chair or even on the floor until he could sort out the problem. They were all still in the dark half an hour later when community police officers arrived to explain that the local electricity substation had been sabotaged by vandals and that theirs was one of over 200 houses in the neighbourhood without power. It was restored an hour and a half later, by which time most of the guests, the catering staff and the string quartet, including the pianist, had groped a way to their vehicles and gone home.

Harry went on to tell me that the next morning he was attending to his first patient downstairs, who not surprisingly was a friend of his wife, the eminent Princess Irma Radnovitchski, when Monique burst into the surgery.

"Harry," she had shouted, "my Transy, she go. She nowhere to be found."

Harry left Irma in the chair and rushed Monique out to the privacy of the kitchen. He returned to the surgery to explain to Her Highness that Moniquc was distressed about her new cat, which had gone missing, and persuaded his patient to come back another day for him to finish the treatment to make her teeth 'dazzlingly white'.

After Irma had left the house all that Harry was able to get out of Monique that made any sense at all was "Darlink, somevun tek it ven ze lights go out, eh?" Monique was referring to her most valuable tiara. To the insurers it was known as the Transylvanian Crown.

"Come on, my love – you weren't wearing it. You were wearing the Ivorski. Nobody but you and I know the code for the wall safe upstairs."

"I forgot put back in safe," she had stammered. "Ven I take her out of safe I remember she so heavy last time I wore – give me neck ache, so no put back in safe. I put in dressing-table drawer. Like you say, I wear the Ivorski instead – is much lighter."

"What!" Harry had shouted at her. "According to the insurers the 'Transy' tiara, as you call it, is worth 17- to 18-million quid at auction. It is the most valuable piece you own. If it was not in the safe and you were not wearing it then it was not insured."

"My darlink, I no care vot it worth. I care it gone."

Harry then told me he promptly consulted his receptionist, who cancelled the rest of his appointments for the day. He then carefully explained to his wife the seriousness of the situation. He told her that they could not report the matter to the police (which is what was required by the insurance company in the event of a claim), not just because they wouldn't pay out anyway if they were told the truth, but because the resulting inevitable publicity would be bound to attract a lot of unwanted attention – most importantly, that of the thieving underworld. "I vill tell them I put back in safe" had been Monique's immediate answer.

"No, no, no," Harry had cried. "Lying to the police will get us into even deeper trouble. Also, just stop and think for a minute. If we tell the police the truth their first thought has to be that it was taken by somebody in the house at the time the lights went out. As there is no evidence of the safe being broken into, all our friends will fall under suspicion and be interrogated, including your pianist boyfriend. Now, that wouldn't be nice, would it?"

"Ze pianist is not my boyfriend" had been Monique's reply.

Harry went on to tell me that he had answered that he was only joking, but told her that because she thought getting her tiara back was more important than getting paid for its loss he had a better idea. He had a patient who owned one of the biggest detective and security agencies in the country. He told Monique that they had operatives all over the world with contacts in every known criminal section. He persuaded her that this man was more likely to find her tiara than anyone. It would thus avoid the embarrassment of having all her friends interrogated by the police and all the undesirable publicity. Horrified at the prospect of the latter, Monique had agreed to Harry's suggestion for recovering her bauble.

At Harry's suggestion she even promised to tell Irma that 'Transy', her cat, had been found and was fine. This would mean that no one who was present that night – except of course the guilty party – would have an inkling that anything other than the cat had gone missing that night.

"This is where you come in, my good friend," Harry said. "Discretion and trust has always been our byword, hasn't it?" Discretion was indeed a top priority of Harry's plan of action.

* * * * * * * * *

A week later a small white van turned into Harry's driveway. A logo on each side panel declared 'T.H.E. Wi-Fi Specialist'. 'T.H.E.' stood for Thomas Henry Everard. Tom, in immaculate white overalls, was not only the owner of the business, but also the company's top sleuth. This is how he introduced himself to Monique. He acknowledged Harry with a nod and the three of them sat down together for a discussion in the privacy of the master bedroom upstairs, where the large wall-safe was cunningly concealed behind a full-length hinged mirror.

Whilst Monique wrote out a list for Tom of all those present at the soirée, which he promised would not go further than the three of them, Harry showed him around the rest of the house, inside and out. An hour or so later he left, calling out to Harry, loud enough for anyone within shouting distance (including the dental receptionist) to hear, something about megabytes per second, fibre cabling and other terms to do with signal strength. He got into his van and drove away.

Tom was next seen at the house a month later during one of Monique's parties, having been invited by Harry.

When he was sure no one else was listening Tom whispered to the lady of the house that progress was being made and he was already confident that her precious heirloom had not left the country. Monique's pleasure was evident.

Another six months passed before Tom turned up again in his van one Sunday and unloaded a pile of paraphernalia that looked like satellite dishes, coils of wire and several cardboard boxes. Monique and Harry helped him to carry it all through to the lounge. Once satisfied that no one else was in the house, Tom delved into one of the boxes.

With a cheesy grin and shouting, "Abracadabra!" he dangled a glittering tiara right in front of Monique's astonished-looking face.

"My Transy!" she screamed. "My darlink, darlink man, how can I tank you? I tort she gone for ever." She took it from him. Tears started to roll down her cheeks as she turned over the sparkling object in her hands and hugged it to her ample bosom. Then she turned to Harry: "Vot you say? You no look surprised."

Harry smiled and kissed her on the cheek.

"Tom told me he was coming, my love. He called me first to tell me the good news. We both wanted to see your face."

"Mrs Naughton," said Tom, looking sheepish, "there is no

need to thank me. My associates and I have been well paid by Mr Naughton. It is all in a day's work for us. This is what we do. What I will say though is that right now, whilst I take these boxes and stuff, which you know is a front for our real activities, back outside, you must take your trinket upstairs immediately and lock it back in the safe. When you come downstairs again, with your permission, Mr Naughton, I would like us to have a little chat."

Five minutes later the three of them were together again. Monique was sat on the sofa holding her husband's hand and looking happy.

"It's like this," said Tom. "Technically a felony has been committed, but the culprit's defence, should anyone attempt a prosecution, would be supported by the fact that the so-called stolen object is still in your possession. You see an argument could be made that borrowing is not stealing. Additionally I myself could be implicated by not reporting its temporary departure. Theft is theft and recovery of stolen goods are two different issues in law."

"But how you do dis ting?" asked Monique.

"We never disclose how we achieve our results. That would give away information to criminals and make it impossible for us to operate the way we do. You also asked that we do not embarrass your friends or even reveal that anything went missing other than the cat that evening when the lights went out. The person who took the tiara is indeed known to you, but I can assure you that they will never reveal themselves or repeat their action. My advice is this: in future keep that object in your excellent wall safe," continued Tom with a wink at Monique, "and never talk of this matter except amongst ourselves. Never – absolutely never ever."

After that, for a few months life continued in much the

same way as usual in the Naughton household except that now Monique did not accompany Harry during his golfing weekends away. This was mutually advantageous – she could indulge more frequently, without his interference, in her 'idle pleasures', and he didn't have to mix with her 'vacuous' friends, as he put it, so often.

Then it happened.

Harry and Monique were in Monaco – unusually, on holiday together – when Harry's dental receptionist, Annabel, phoned them one morning to say that the house had been entered during the night and that she had found their upstairs wall safe open. They flew straight back that day. The police were still crawling all over the place when they arrived late in the afternoon. It seemed from the CCTV recordings that only one masked and hooded person, clearly with full knowledge of their security devices and combinations, had arrived on foot and entered via the front door without activating any alarms.

Annabel was supposed to be the only person other than themselves who had the knowledge of how to enter in this way. The door from the surgery through to their living area was protected by a combination lock. It was this door that Annabel had found open when she arrived in the morning to deal with the mail and her boss's future appointments, etc. Naturally she first called the police immediately she had discovered the wall safe open upstairs, and then she phoned her boss.

Monique's habit of taking nearly all her valuable jewellery with her wherever she went made it easy for the Naughtons to tell the police what was missing when they all went up to the bedroom. Nothing – except the Transy.

Not for the first time, Monique screamed, "My Transy, my Transy, she gone!"

Under the guise of comforting his wife, Harry whispered in her ear, "Not a word about the first time, remember."

It took the police only a few days to conclude, not only the obvious – that it was an inside job – but also that, as a result of an anonymous tip-off, the only fingerprints all over the bedroom other than Monique's and Harry's were those of the young piano player. His fingerprints were identifiable from the piano keyboard. Nor did it take Harry very long to declare that this man could only have been in their bedroom at the invitation of his wife.

Harry filed for divorce. Everyone considered that the settlement to Monique of half a million quid was extremely generous, considering she was allowed to keep the rest of her precious heirlooms. Harry's charge of adultery was incontestable. The charges against Monique and her lover for conspiring to commit a robbery were dropped by mutual consent when the 'thief' gave the 'stolen' tiara back to the owner and she went off to live with him.

It is said that fortune favours the bold. How fortunate that Harry had read in the press that my company had made the replicas that were stolen from the Tower of London! How fortunate that this came to Harry's mind the night the lights went out! How fortunate that the power failure came when it did! How fortunate that Harry had not taken any action earlier on the night the lights went out when he'd noticed Monique put the Transy in the drawer in the bedroom instead of returning it to the safe!

The time has come for me to explain myself. Many years ago I found that the delicate work of mounting gems into precious metal was similar to dentistry in its dexterity, but much more exciting than poking around inside people's mouths. I had also discovered a secret process for producing synthetic gems, which made it much cheaper to make them than hitherto, and they still looked every bit as real. The snag that had only revealed itself recently was that the sparkle that made them look indistinguishable from the genuine article could not be guaranteed beyond twenty years or so.

Once this information was known, gems produced this way would be much cheaper in the marketplace, but the costs in my laboratory and what we had to pay the industry's top gemstone cutters could not be reduced. The future of my company's viability was dubious.

And so it had taken nearly six months for my company to make the replica Transy tiara from the original 'borrowed' by Harry. All my staff have signed non-disclosure agreements in order to protect owners from this well-known method of foiling thieves. We cut and set the synthetic gems into the original gold-and-silver frame. The original genuine diamonds (the single centrepiece diamond alone was thirty carats) together with the emeralds fetched a net £15 million in Brazil. Split three ways, happiness all round!

How come *three* ways?

Harry got his pension fund, and rid of a millstone round his neck. The pianist (poor chap – only Harry knew the 5 million quid he paid him wouldn't last them a lifetime) naturally kept his silence after his one and only venture into burglary. He'd never seen so much money in all his life, and of course he had his new love, and she had her Transy back. As for myself, alias Thomas Henry Everard, I was now able to fulfil my own retirement plans.

Fair exchange, it is said, is no robbery.

HMP
PARKHURST
AROMAPHONE

A WHIFF OF SUCCESS

Arthur F. Smart lived on the Isle of Wight, UK, and was known to his friends as Smart Art. He sold over 7 million of his SuperSmart mobile phones, which he called Aromaphones, before the complaints rolled in. The USP (unique selling point) for this widely advertised device was that the owner could send a message which when opened would release a fragrance of the sender's choice. To experience this miracle of modern data technology, the recipient also had to own an Aromaphone.

Fred, who a few years ago had shared a cell with Smart Art in Parkhurst Prison, Isle of Wight, was one of Art's earliest customers.

"That's something you didn't tell me, you crafty old bastard," complained Fred in his call to Art.

"Well, I would have thought it was bleeding obvious," retorted Art, not well known for his finesse.

This was how Art lost his few friends rapidly, and why he also saw reason to flee the country. For it only took just two more months after the initial launch for Art to antagonise millions more, who believed the advertising and wanted to be the first to send their friends a smelly message.

Of course none of the recipients of new Aromaphones wanted to appear foolish after reading in the instructions that their plan wouldn't work unless these friends also had one. Yet again Art had pulled off another scam.

By the time worldwide sales had reached 10 million it was generally accepted that sending smells by phone was the 'Art' of the impossible. By the time the Fraud Squad in London were on the trail, neither Arthur Smart nor the manufacturer in the Far East could be traced.

Now, Fred had shared a cell at Parkhurst Prison, Isle of Wight, not only with Art, but also with Harry. Harry, since his release, was now going straight and had a job with the Fraud Squad, doing what he did best – cracking codes and encryptions, and hacking into the World Wide Web. Fred phoned Harry to tell him all about it.

"Harry, me old mate, my guess is that you've got all the gear there. If anyone can make this thing work I guess it's you. We both know that old Art didn't get his nickname for nothing."

The Metropolitan Police had an algorithm in their computer system that searched criminal records for connections to be made to names or activities. A few days after Fred's phone call, Harry, after everyone else had left work for home, entered '*Arthur F. Smart (now known as Smelly Art), believed from Cowes, Isle of Wight*'. The application came up with a sequence of numbers, which he then tapped into an Aromaphone his department had acquired, '3 – 15 – 23 – 19 – 8 – 9 – 20', followed by pressing 'control' and 'function'.

After seeing the cartoon of a steaming cowpat with 'Ha! Ha! Art' beneath it on the screen, Harry, fearful of being laughed out of his job, breaking his terms of parole and any chance of future employment, trashed his entry, shredded the Aromaphone's chip and never muttered a single word about his discovery.

Would you?

SHAME

At first, to me, it looked like a bundle of old clothes, swept up on to the ledge by last night's high tide. As I clambered over the rocks for a closer look I noticed a movement – perhaps a gust had disturbed it. There was no wind. I hastened my steps up toward the steep cliff face. Now I could see blood – not just on the bundle of clothes, but congealed on the rocks – and a tangled pile of arms and legs that was a human being.

I knelt to peer at the face of an old man. An eyelid flickered; his lips moved. I could not hear what he was saying, but he clearly could see me through half-open eyes. I tilted my head closer to his face.

"I am so ashamed," he rasped, and then groaned in pain.

I reached for my phone, praying that the signal could be picked up from the base of such a high cliff in such an isolated location. It could, but in just those few minutes before I turned again to see what more I could do for him, this bloody heap of human wreckage had departed this world.

As I sat beside him and wept I heard the sound of the maroon from the little harbour a mile away from where I had started out that morning. I knew that immediately busy people would be dropping whatever they were doing to rush to the lifeboat house, and they'd soon be on their way to the place I had described. As I looked down at what was now no longer a figure of pain and anguish, I consoled myself with the knowledge that at least he was finally at peace with himself.

Back at the local police station I was grateful for the cup of tea they brought me as they took down my report of the events of that morning. Grateful also for the lift back to my little cottage not far from the top of those same high cliffs, hundreds of feet below which I had witnessed the result of an avoidable tragedy. Just how do I know it was avoidable? you ask. I will tell you.

You see, I knew the man in question. I could not tell you his name. He never told me. I never asked. We met at the nursing home where we visited our respective wives, who each suffered from being banged up in a high-sided bed 24/7, unable to do much for themselves due to one evil disease or another. Us two old men exchanged very few words when we met at the home occasionally. Our attention was directed totally to bringing as much comfort as we could to our partners.

On one occasion as we were passing in the corridor he was looking sad so I had said to him, "We do what we can."

I shuddered then at his reply: "You might," he said, "but I have failed."

How I wish now that I had said to him what my father had said to me eighty years previously when I failed my exams: "There is no shame in failure, my son. Shame relates only to those who do not try."

WELCOME B.A.B.Y. BAKER

A BAKER'S DOZEN

You'd be entitled to think that the Bakers must have been paralytically pissed when in 1917 they named their son Brayden Aiden Bentley York Baker – B. A. B. Y. Baker. Yes, they did just that. And yes, they were out of their minds. It took eighteen years before Ben could legally change his name himself. By then, because of the experience of his childhood, he had become a unique character. And yes, I mean *unique*.

"In what way?" you would be entitled to ask.

Well, he has just been turned down by the *Famous Book of Records* on the grounds, they say, that the claim he has put to them, whilst being admittedly irrefutable, would be a grave danger to the health of millions of people were they to publish it. How could this be? Read on.

His claim was that extensive medical examination of the organs of his body and his declaration concerning his consumption of alcohol since birth indicated that he had proved that he had become immune from the effects of alcohol on his longevity. In fact, there were eminent physicians prepared to swear that such ingestion might even increase his lifespan.

Much too much was going on during and just after the First World War for anyone to take a lot of notice of a story that appeared in the back pages of a British West

Country provincial newspaper around that time about a couple who were taken to court for lacing their baby's feeding bottle with alcohol. They were charged with neglect. The case was dismissed for lack of evidence, the only evidence being that Mrs Baker, inebriated at the time, had told someone in the pub that she occasionally put 'a drop of gin' in her baby's bottle 'to help him sleep'.

Pat and Fred Baker, the couple in question, were known and liked for miles around. Their smallholding on the edge of a little North Somerset village sold eggs and fresh vegetables to the only shop in that tiny isolated community. There were many more horses to be seen than motor vehicles in those days on the only minor road that passed through this sleepy place. Fred's van was on that road most days. Fred had a finger in every pie, as they used to say. He supplied the Wagon and Horses, as well as other pubs and outlets for miles around, with beers, wines, spirits and tobacco from his many contacts in the city of Bristol, just a few miles to the north, such as Georges Brewery, Harveys Wine Merchants, W. D. & H. O Wills (tobacco), and also from the fruit and vegetable markets there.

About eighteen years later, when Fred and Pat were found dead in bed, the public were more interested in the rise of a certain Adolf Hitler than the report in the same local rag that said that what led to their death was most likely that they had consumed four bottles of gin between them on the day previous to the discovery of their bodies. They had been with their son celebrating his eighteenth birthday in the Wagon and Horses. The three of them were last seen staggering home after the pub closed at ten o'clock that night. By the time the vicar found the bodies the next day, the son, Ben, had vanished.

A coroner's inquest decided that liver failure was the cause of death. The acute cirrhosis that both suffered from was revealed and nobody was surprised at the verdict. Those with some medical experience were pleased that such a smart lad as Ben would probably know that a sudden death from what was then called an 'affliction' can in reality be painless, so villagers believed that he had simply run off to start a new life. There was absolutely no evidence to the contrary, and young Ben had often talked about wanting to see more of the world.

This quiet Somerset village where the Baker family had lived for generations was a close-knit community. Most of the villagers met together in the church on a Sunday, and even more often in the Wagon and Horses most days of the week. The drinking habits of the village population were not a conversation piece for any of them, and the strange diet with which the Baker family had nurtured their son for years was all but forgotten. After all, they could see what a fine, strong and clever lad he'd turned out to be.

Despite the bullying at school in the early days because of his initials, Ben enjoyed a happy childhood. He had grown at a faster rate than most and was as strong as an ox. He not only learned how fists can beat bullying, but was top of the class in all subjects as well and clearly headed for great things. Then he vanished. At first the local police took an interest in the coincidence of his disappearance and his parents' deaths. However, it was the vicar who satisfied them beyond doubt that his reaction was a perfectly natural one. But the vicar was disturbed. He had not told them everything he knew about the affair.

You see, the incumbent at the time of the Bakers' deaths was the same priest who had presided at the christening of their only child. It was not until after this ceremony, and when he had sat down in the vestry to complete the necessary paperwork, that it dawned on him what he had done. Even then, at first, it seemed quite cute to call a child 'Baby'. But as the child grew older the vicar felt more and more that he should have tried before the baptism to dissuade the parents from those names, especially in that order. He even comforted himself with knowing that he had encouraged the boy to use the name Ben. Now this fine young man – like his parents, a regular churchgoer and one of his parishioners – had gone missing. Our trusted man of the cloth was prevented by his faith from revealing any matters that he had been told in confidence.

* * * * * * * * * *

In 1967 Colonel Benjamin Smith, MD, of the United States Medical Corps was at home reading, as he always did, 'Notes from England' in his newspaper. One day he read that Her Majesty the Queen had honoured the vicar of a small obscure Somerset parish with the Most Noble Order of the Garter (KG). The article went on to explain that Britain's highest honour was for service to the nation and to the church after fifty years in the same parish, during which five years were spent in the British Army during the Second World War, mostly in war zones, where he had been awarded the Military Cross.

Also in 1967 the Very Reverend Harold Smith, MC, now aged seventy-two, was reminded during his visit to Buckingham Palace of his moral responsibilities. The motto that went with the Most Noble Order he received was '*Honi soit qui mal y pense*.'(Evil be to him who evil thinks.)

Colonel Benjamin Smith sought leave from his unit and took the next possible plane to the UK. He drove his hire car straight to the Somerset village where he was born. He was still in his uniform as he removed his cap and entered the little church he had attended for eighteen years. There was the font he'd last seen in 1935, when he was seventeen years of age. Thirty-two years later, hoping to find the man he was seeking, he looked around. The vestry door was locked.

He called out aloud, "Anyone there?"

'You fool,' he said to himself, 'go to the pub.'

He drove into the car park next to the Wagon and Horses. He remembered this area as an orchard when he was a lad. Where the entrance to the off-licence shop used to be there was now a brick-built one-storey extension with a notice over the door that said 'Restaurant'. In other respects the pub looked just the same from the outside as he remembered. Inside he found what he had come for.

At a corner table sat a clean-shaven ruddy-faced old man with a half-full pint beer mug. The dog collar was the clue. Colonel Smith made straight for the table, pulled up a spare chair and sat down, elbows on the table, chin resting in his hands as he faced the man in front of him.

"Well, Rev," he said, "how're you doing these days?"

"Do I know you?" quizzed the old man.

"No, you don't," said the Yank, "but you used to."

"What sort of an answer is that?" replied the vicar as he peered into the face opposite.

"The sort that has taken thirty-two years and 6,000 miles to give."

Ben's face broadened into a smile as he held out his hand, and after what seemed like minutes he saw tears start to roll down the old man's cheeks.

Back at the vicarage, which was in a state of shambles, with rolled-up carpets, bare floors and packing cases everywhere, Ben and the old man sat facing each other on either side of the ancient scrubbed oak kitchen table. Tomorrow the removal vans were coming.

Following the death of his wife three years earlier the vicar had talked of retiring and going to live with his sister in the neighbouring county of Dorset. Now the diocese had made up his mind for him. They had 'suggested' that his curate was more suitable for the task of looking after the five churches in an area that had grown to nearly 200 square miles, as opposed to the one church when he was first ordained. With falling church attendances and reduced finances, they made it clear that the stipend could no longer support two people where one younger and more energetic would now suffice.

"Why, Ben, has it taken you so long to come back?" enquired the old man. "Not a card, not a word. You had friends. People cared. I cared. Thirty-two years have passed and you breeze in as if it were only yesterday."

"Rev, I'm very, very sorry. I was scared. I ran away. I took what I thought was mine anyway, then I thought the British police might not see it that way. Ever since, in my new life in America I have been in fear of being extradited back to England – in fear of losing everything I've worked so hard for over the last thirty-two years. Now I've come to beg you for your forgiveness."

"My son," said the old man, and his eyes turned moist

again, "it is me that should be doing the begging."

He reached for the phone and dialled the pub number.

Following the death of the vicar's wife the landlord of the Wagon and Horses had, being a faithful parishioner, sent a meal round to the vicarage whenever the old boy had asked.

"Best takeaway for miles," the vicar once said aloud during one of his not infrequent visits to the pub.

"Sh-h-h," the landlord had replied, "or everyone will want a home delivery."

Since that episode the vicar had changed his tune. "After all," he was often heard to say as if to justify his daily visits, "how else am I going to settle my account?"

On this particular night the meal delivered to the vicarage was for two. Ben and the Very Reverend Harold Smith sat at the old kitchen table enjoying their supper together, washed down with a bottle of Beaujolais, as they reminisced. Then they cleared away the dirty dishes and, with an apology from the Reverend for having to use the wine glasses again, they opened the bottle of gin, which also miraculously appeared from the Reverend's packed boxes, along with the tonic water, as had the wine earlier.

Ben's Tale

"The one thing that Dad drummed into me all my life was never to trust banks or lawyers. I know it sounds silly today, but in those days he wasn't the only one. He told me that you, Rev, were the only person other than myself who knew that he and Mum kept all their savings in an old tea chest in the storeroom next to the stable outside.

"When I found them looking so peaceful in death I

don't know what came over me. That tea chest in the outhouse had packets of tea in a compartment in the top. But hidden beneath its false floor was all that money – thousands of pounds in ten- and twenty-pound notes. I took the lot, packed my bag and legged it over the fields. That afternoon I was on a train from Bristol to Liverpool."

Ben, encouraged by the old man and the gin, warmed to his story of how he had landed on his feet, so to speak, from the moment he arrived at Liverpool Railway Station. He had gone to the enquiries window at the railway station and asked where he could book a passage to New York and where he might find comfortable accommodation whilst waiting to sail. His luck was in. The clerk he spoke to picked up the phone, had a brief conversation with the person who answered, and directed him to his wife's lodging house a short distance away. They had been putting up people bent on the same purpose as Ben for many years.

Emigration to America had been a significant part of the economy in Liverpool for decades. This couple listened sympathetically as he told them truthfully that his parents had died suddenly, of his desire to change his name, the reason why, and the hope as had hundreds of thousands before him of a better life on the other side of the Atlantic.

The mention of his 'inheritance', which would pay for this new start encouraged his new friends to look after him well. They were also able to guide him to the right places in town, where he could achieve all his immediate objectives.

Ben was amazed at just how easy it was to change his name by deed poll, and delighted to discover that he did not need a lawyer to make a statutory change of name. Pleased again when he was able to buy a cabin passage on a ship named MV *Georgic*, which was making its last passage on the Liverpool to New York route the following week.

And so Benjamin Oswald Samuel Smith set out for the New World with a new name – one which he thought might help his anonymity – and initials he had chosen carefully to boost his confidence. With new clothes, and his money, now changed into United States dollars hidden in the lining of his leather and secure cabin trunk, he headed for the Liverpool Docks.

The opulence of the ship's first-class accommodation (a lower deck or steerage ticket was not available at such short notice) amazed him. Within a couple of days he was invited by an American man and his wife to join them and their daughter at their table in the dining saloon. They were of Jewish extraction, and because of terrible stories coming from Europe about the Nazi's treatment of Jews they had come over to bring Carol, their daughter, back from her education in England.

It was love at first sight for Ben. Carol's father was a surgeon at the New York Hospital in Manhattan. They took to Ben – tall, handsome, and smart – from the moment he told them his story. Seven days later, at the end of the passage, Ben's future was cast. They sponsored his American citizenship. They gave him a home in their spare bedroom and oiled the wheels that got both Ben and Carol into Cornell University. In 1941 these two young people celebrated their medical degrees (MD) by getting married. Both went to the New York Hospital for their internships, at the end of which they were abruptly separated because of Ben's decision.

Carol continued as a physician at the New York Hospital, but Ben had decided to join the United States

Medical Corps. He was promptly sent to Houston, Texas – 1,600 miles away! For he had another objective: to get to England and help the fight to defend his country of origin. However, the military had other ideas. You see, Ben's career and lifestyle profile fitted their urgent need for specialist researchers.

On passing his personal medical examination for entry into the US military, Ben had revealed to the doctor who discussed the result with him that he had been weaned on gin since the day he was born. Not only did that information raise the doctor's eyebrows, but Ben also told him that he couldn't remember a single day in his life when he hadn't consumed alcohol.

Now, not only did the Americans not approve of the British tradition of splicing the mainbrace, but they were having problems with increasing absenteeism of members of their armed services due to alcoholism.

For those not familiar with the term 'splicing the mainbrace', it should be remembered that for hundreds of years the 'courage' of the British Navy was officially strengthened by the ritual consumption of rum at critical times of danger and enterprise.

Ben continued his narrative:

"Rev, my old friend, if I may call you that, from thereon my future as a servant of the United States was guaranteed. They put me personally through vigorous physical tests. They opened a new physiology department with me at the head to map and study every organ of the body for the effects of alcohol on human behaviour and longevity.

"Many times I was tempted to give them your name so as to corroborate the facts that I had given them about my own life experience from birth, but it wasn't necessary despite the fact that several of their top guys endorsed my thesis. The subject became academic after hundreds of mice died of organ failure of some sort or another in tests. They simply were not prepared to seek real people who had been weaned on alcohol to take part in clinical trials."

"But, Ben, my dear boy," said the Reverend Smith, "what was all this business you were telling me earlier about not writing your memoirs?"

"Aha!" replied Ben. "Not so long ago I decided to write my memoirs after a learned colleague of mine had told me I could make a fortune from my story. So I wrote to the publishers of the *Famous Book of Records* in the belief that they might be a good place to start for advice on how to set about it."

A frown came over the Reverend's face.

"What's the problem, Rev?" asked Ben.

"Carry on, Ben. I'll tell you later."

"Well, the guy I spoke to in England on the blower – at his expense, I might say – seemed very interested and naturally wanted to know if I could corroborate my story. I think I said I could if the vicar of my parish in Somerset at the time was still around. At that point I began to think that I had already said too much and decided that I would not give him your name when he asked. I realised that it would only be plain courtesy to ask you for your permission first."

"Which, I take it, Ben, is why you are here right now?"

"Yes."

The Reverend Smith staggered across to one of the packing cases and produced another bottle of gin and more tonic water.

"We have a problem, young Ben . . ."

But before he could finish his sentence Ben interrupted him: "Rev, please, I am very tired and must find myself somewhere to stay tonight. Can we continue this conversation tomorrow?"

"Shhgood idea, young Ben. You shall stay here. Not another word. We still have bedrooms and beds and hot and cold water. Go get your bags," he said, waving his hand in the direction of Ben's car outside. "I will postpone my move to Dorset tomorrow and I will seek guidance in the morning. We have some very important matters to discuss."

Ben knew that he should not be driving his car after all the booze, and slept well that night on a comfortable bed way up on the top floor of the old vicarage. He had the bathroom to himself in the morning. He found a note on the kitchen table telling him how to find all the stuff for his breakfast, but there was no sign of the old boy.

"I have put off my move until tomorrow," announced the Reverend Smith as he came through the front door and entered the kitchen. "I have made my peace with my Maker and sought His guidance. I have thanked Him for reuniting us. Indeed, the Lord most certainly works in mysterious ways His wonders to perform."

Silence prevailed for a little while after this speech whilst Ben thought carefully about his response. 'Pompous old sod hasn't changed a bit,' he thought to himself, but, brought up as a dutiful follower of the Church of England and remembering that he was a guest of a servant of that faith and an old man he respected so much that he had chosen to take his name, he bit his tongue.

"Rev," he answered, " before we go any further, whilst I have told you what has happened to me these last thirty years or so please remember that I am married to a Jew."

"I know, Ben. I know much more than you realise. This is why I ask you to sit at the table this morning and let me tell you something that will make your memoirs memorable. Firstly, Ben, I would like you to call me Harold."

Ben nodded in agreement.

"Secondly, whatever our faith, we all believe in the same God. I also believe that you and I value the truth above all else."

Ben nodded again.

"Then let us get the coffee flowing this time, pull up a chair, and interrupt me at any point where you require clarification. It is clear to me now, Ben, that the same person who phoned you from the *Famous Book of Records* is the one who phoned me. He did not mention that he had spoken to you. All he said was that his 'informant' in America had traced a 'relative' of mine. As there are millions of Smiths in the world, such a statement did not arouse my interest and I told him so. However, he went on to say that for that very reason I ought to be interested, particularly if the person is a very close relative. So, Ben, before anybody digs any further into our private affairs and adds two and two to make five – and to put the record straight – here goes."

The Reverend Smith's Tale

"When I officiated at your mum and dad's wedding in our little church I was only a couple of years into my first paid job since my ordination. They became my best friends as I got to know my parishioners. They had welcomed me into their lives, invited me into their own parents' homes. They were already deeply in love when I took up residence, and one of the earliest couples for whom I solemnised the holy state of marriage.

"What has worried me after listening to your story, dear Ben, flattered though I am, is that the choice for a new name that you made thirty two years ago may add strength to a malicious rumour that was put about in this parish some fifty years ago."

"For God's sake, Rev – sorry, Harold – what on earth are you talking about?" Ben managed to restrain himself from completing his sentence with 'you pompous ass'.

Among Fred Baker's earliest influential contacts in Bristol just after the First World War was a professor of medicine at the newly opened Department for Veterinary and Medical Studies at the University of Bristol. Fred had been introduced to this eminent individual by his contact at W. D. & H. O. Wills, the large tobacco-products company founded in Bristol. Among many benefits this company had provided for a century or more was free medical care for its hundreds of mainly female employees. This company had recently endowed the newly formed university with considerable finance for research. It seems that Fred, in his desperation, mentioned to the Professor that he and his wife wanted to have a child, but after two years of trying they were beginning to think that something was wrong with one or both of them.

At this point in the old man's narrative Ben interrupted: "Harold, to save you any embarrassment, I can tell you that I know about that rumour you just mentioned. It was initiated by a girl my father knew before he had even met

Mum. This girl felt that she had been jilted, and out of spite she spread the story that because my father was infertile my mum must have had a boyfriend to become pregnant."

"I take it you never believed that?" was Harold's reply.

"Not for one moment."

"Then your choice of a new surname name for yourself came from respect for me?"

"Absolutely. . . ."

Ben's voice trailed away as he raised his eyebrows and stared at the other man with a look of astonishment. Harold recognised that moment.

"Fear not, my friend," he said. "I may be guilty of withholding information, but I could not maintain my faith by not telling the truth. That is why I sought guidance early this morning from my Boss (and here he smiled, remembering Ben's new initials) as you would have me call Him. As a man of medicine yourself, you will recognise the truth; and the story I tell you may not produce the fortune that you are looking for, but it will bring its own reward. The person who spread that pernicious and vengeful rumour is still alive, but all the others involved in what at the time was considered illegal by some have departed this world. Your book must shine light on the truth. Somewhere deep in the archives in Bristol will be buried my sworn affidavit."

Ben was certain that despite the old boy's imperious delivery of these words he was about to hear something he did not know – and a truth.

More coffee was called for.

"Your dad told me about his contact at the new university. The learned professor was concerned in his everyday job with the improvement of breeding programmes for farm animals. After a long discussion with your father he proposed that if Fred and Mrs Baker would secretly offer themselves for artificial insemination, and if, as he suspected, Fred was not infertile but had a physical problem with his reproductive tract, then the chances of them having a child were extremely high.

"Your mum and dad came to me for advice. The part I played in the joyous outcome lies in the affidavit I mentioned. I was witness to the absolute certainty during the procedure that Fred Baker was your biological father. All of us involved put our signatures to that document.

"At the time we were not sure that we were acting legally, but I knew then, and you sitting here with me now confirms it, that we were acting for the benefit of all concerned as well as mankind. DNA testing, although a recent development, will now not only scotch any surviving rumour but enable you to claim in the *Famous Book of Records* to be the first baby born by artificial insemination. How's that for being unique?"